Falling for The Wrong Hustla

3

Facebook Author T M Jenkins

D1468901

More books from me:

The Thug I Chose 1, 2 & 3

A Thin Line Between Me and My Thug 1 & 2

I Got Luv For My Shawty 1 & 2

Kharis and Caleb: A Different Kind of Love 1 & 2

Loving You Is A Battle 1 & 2 & 3

Violet and The Connect 1 & 2 & 3

We Both End Up With Scars

You Complete Me

Love Will Lead You Back

This Thing Called Love

Are We In This Together 1,2 &3

Shawty Down To Ride For a Boss 1, 2 &3

When A Boss Falls in Love 1, 2 & 3

Let Me Be The One 1 & 2

We Got That Forever Love

Aint No Savage Like The One I Got 1&2

A Queen and A Hustla 1, 2 & 3

Thirsty For A Bad Boy 1&2

Hassan and Serena: An Unforgettable Love 1&2

Still Luvin A Beast 1&2

Her Man, His Savage 1 & 2

Marco & Rakia: Not Your Ordinary, Hood Kinda
Love 1,2 & 3

Feenin For A Real One 1, 2 & 3

A Kingpin's Dynasty 1, 2 & 3

What Kinda Love Is This: Captivating A Boss 1, 2 & 3

Frankie & Lexi: Luvin A Young Beast 1, 2 & 3

A Dope Boys Seduction 1, 2 & 3

My Brother's Keeper 1, 2 & 3

C'Yani & Meek: A Dangerous Hood Love 1, 2 & 3

When A Savage Falls for A Good Girl 1, 2 & 3

Eva & Deray 1 & 2

A Beast Christmas

Blame It On His Gangsta Luv 1, 2 & 3

Falling for The Wrong Hustla 1 & 2

<u>*Warning:*</u>

This book is strictly Urban Fiction and the story is

<u>NOT REAL</u>!

Characters will not behave the way you want them to; nor will they react to situations the way you think they should. Some of them may be drug addicts, kingpins, savages, thugs, rich, poor, ho's, sluts, haters, bitter ex-girlfriends or boyfriends, people from the past and the list can go on and on. That is what Urban Fiction mostly consists of. If this isn't anything you foresee yourself interested in, then do yourself a favor and don't read it because it's only going to piss you off. □□

Also, the book will not end the way you want so please be advised that the outcome will be based solely on my own thoughts and ideas. I hope you enjoy this book. Thanks so much to my readers, supporters, publisher and fellow authors and authoress for the support. □□

Table of Contents

Ivan

"Your rude ass father damn near bit my head off when he saw me. Then, he threw the suitcase and bags on the ground and told me hell no he wasn't helping me put them in the car. And that was after he told me off and called me a whore." Nelly explained in detail the things that took place when she stopped by my parents.

I could've gone myself but then we would've been arguing and I'm over them. Plus, my brother was there and if he found out what I did and said to my mother, it's no doubt in my mind he'd kill me. He's always been the baby outta us and regardless of the money he gave me, it doesn't make him better.

"Then, Remi said you had two days to have the rent or we getting kicked out. Ivan what's going on because I was under the assumption you had money."

"I do." I lifted my beer to drink.

"He says you don't and the accountant who handled your affairs has been terminated." She revealed new information to me because no one told me.

I mean yea, Remi has always been in charge of the money he dispensed to me, but his accountant never questioned what it was needed for. If he fired him it means I can't do what I want with the remaining money I have, unless Remi approves it.

"Nelly did you really stick around for the money?" I don't know what made me ask.

"Ivan, you of all people should know the answer to your own question." She rose up off the couch and I grabbed her wrist.

"If I did, I wouldn't ask." She sat back down and looked at me.

"Ivan we've been sleeping with each other off and on for years. You've been with other woman and I've been with other men. You've funded my lifestyle and I appreciate it but if you're broke, I have to move on." I nodded my head.

"Do you regret choosing me over Remi?"

"Actually yes. Remi was good to me as a friend before we even slept together. I only wanted to be with an older guy because my friends were. Then you taught me things in the bedroom and started giving me money. I wasn't gonna pass up anything; especially, when you offered without me asking."

"I see." I didn't know if I should be mad or respect her hustle.

"I've experienced other men and sadly, in the beginning I couldn't handle how big they were after being with you for so long."

"What the fuck you tryna say?"

"Ivan don't play as if you don't know your dick is below average size." She rolled her eyes.

"Why continue sleeping with me then?"

"I just told you. The money kept me here and I'm not saying the sex is bad. I'm saying after being with others I noticed the difference."

"All these years my family said you were using me, and I didn't listen."

"You should've. Most people can tell." She shrugged her shoulders.

"Ok." I said and put my beer on the coffee table.

We're not in love or anything like that but I did believe she had some feelings for me. I mean damn! We've been together all these years and I'm just learning it was for the money. Maybe, I was in denial but whatever the case, she fucked with the wrong dude and today is gonna be her first lesson. Never fuck with a person's feelings or stick around with for the wrong reasons.

WHAP! WHAP! I smacked her over and over.

"IVAN STOP!" She started kicking at me and I moved each time.

"Get out!" I grabbed her hair and literally drug her out the house.

I opened the door and she began to scream. I pulled her back in, stomped on her face a few times and continued kicking her again. The screaming stopped, which made me look and Nelly appeared to be dead.

I went upstairs, changed my shoes because there was blood on them and left the house with her inside. The bitch thought she had one up on me. I bet she doesn't anymore.

****

"Is your husband home?" I asked my mother on the phone. She's been asking me to stop by so we could talk about what happened.

"No. Are you here?" I noticed the shade go up in the living room and soon the door opened. I stepped out my car and surveyed the area to be sure my father or Remi wasn't pulling up.

"Hey Ivan. I missed you so much." She hugged me and it was pure torture to return the embrace. I loved my mother, but I also know where her allegiance lies and it ain't with me.

"Do you have anything to eat?" I moved passed and walked straight in the kitchen.

"There's some meatloaf in there and the sides are in Tupperware." I grabbed a plate from the cabinet and began opening the different containers to make me a plate.

"Ivan, I want to talk to you about…"

"DAMN MA. CAN I MAKE MY FUCKING PLATE FIRST?" I shouted making her jump. She put her hands up in surrender. I placed my food in the microwave and turned around.

"Not so tough when your husband isn't here."

"Son, I don't wanna fight with you. I'll wait for you to finish." She took a seat at the table after making a cup of coffee.

BEEP! BEEP! The microwave went off. I removed my plate, grabbed some silverware and sat down. Remembering I had nothing to drink, I hopped up and took a soda out. My mother stared at me with concern, sadness and disappointment on her face. It angered me and I snapped.

"What the fuck are you looking at?" I started antagonizing her because no one was here. I wanted to see if she'd pop off at the mouth like before when my father was home.

"What do you want Ivan? Is it money? Is it attention? Just tell me so I can make you happy. I hate this distance and bad energy surrounding this family." I ignored her.

"IVAN STEVENS! DON'T YOU DARE IGNORE ME."

"Or what?" I looked up at her.

"Or what huh?" I dropped my fork and pushed my chair out.

"You know what? This was a bad idea and it's time for you to go." We were both standing, and I give it to my mother, she refused to back down.

"I'm not going anywhere. You offered me food and I'm gonna finish it." I went to sit back down and felt hot liquid going down the back of my neck.

"What the fuck?"

"Get outta my house." She had her arms folded and it pissed me off to see she wasn't worried about anything. I walked towards her and she moved back.

WHAP! I backhanded the shit outta her. The force swung her body around and she caught herself from falling by gripping the countertop.

"That's for the last time you put your hands on me. Whew! It felt good too." I shook my neck and jumped up and down.

"You wanna fight? Ok." She used her thumb to clean the blood leaking from her lip.

"Ahhhhh." I never saw her leg lift but her kick to the balls was on point. I dropped to my knees giving her full access to do whatever.

"I told you before, my sons will respect me."

WHAP! She smacked and punched me over and over. I couldn't even stop her because my dick was in a lotta pain.

"Now. Like I said, get the fuck…" She tried to say. I mustered up enough energy to grab her leg. She hit the ground and her other foot was kicking me in the face, but I still didn't let go.

"Let me go." She tried to release herself from me. I was finally able to get up and lifted her by the hair.

"I'm going to have to beat your ass the same way I did Nelly." I banged her face into the wall on the way out the kitchen and heard her nose crack or break.

"You think because you're my mother, I'm supposed to be ok with the way you speak or put your hands on me? Nah. I'm not built that way." I continued dragging her up the steps by the hair, with her nose bleeding and her screaming.

"Get me the money out your safe." I tossed her on the floor in her bedroom. She held her nose and pressed her back against the bed.

"Ok fine. What's the combination?" Her crying started getting on my nerves.

"SHUT THAT FUCKING CRYING UP!" I yelled in her face and demanded the combination again. I was aggravated when she said it was my birthday. That's dumb; especially since she hates me.

The safe opened and there had to be at least a million dollars in it. I grabbed a duffle bag from the side of the closet and placed all of it inside. I closed it back and stared at my mother lying in a fetal position in front of the bed.

"Let's get this over with." She looked at me with fear. Blood still gushing out and her face was turning pale.

"It has to appear to be a break in and then an accident." I shrugged and drug her by the feet out the room.

"NO IVAN. LET GO!" She shouted and it fell on deaf ears. Her hands were grasping at the rails of the steps.

"Don't worry. The fall won't be too hard."

"What?"

"When you die, I'm sure your insurance policy will pay me a lot."

"Ivan please don't do this."

"You have to die because if not, you'll tell that husband and son of yours. They'll kill me and I can't have that. I'm just getting started."

"Please Ivan." Her begging started getting on my nerves.

"No need to beg and you're dying anyway. I mean look at all the blood on the ground. Why delay the inevitable?" The look on her face was priceless. Now she'll see how it feels when someone has you at a disadvantage like my father did when he choked me, or the many times Remi beat my ass.

"And down goes Frazier." I laid her in front of the steps and used my foot to push her. I watched her body roll down the hard-wooden stairs and smiled. It had to hurt and once she hit bottom and didn't move, I felt my job here was done.

I reached the bottom of the steps and kneeled down. Unfortunately, she wasn't dead but by the shallow breaths she took, I knew her time was coming. I kneeled down next to her and lifted her head.

"I told you to leave me the fuck alone. You should've never allowed me back in the same house you kicked me out of dumb bitch."

BAM! I slammed her face into the ground. There was no sound which again, led me to believe she's on her way out. All I have to do is wait for the call and cash in my policy. Life is good.

Naima

"Wow! It came out so nice." I gushed to Remi about the kitchen in my house.

It's been three weeks since Mario returned it and it didn't resemble anything like before. The floors were all different, the paint color changed in every room and the kitchen is like one out of a magazine. Remi even had the back deck re-done and added a BBQ pit. It made me think freaky sex isn't anywhere near enough to compensate for the money he most likely put out.

"You must be crazy if you thought I'd leave remnants of any man in here. Yo ass won't be reminiscing about anyone except me." He had me against the wall with his hand over my head.

"Remi this is nice and way too much money. Let me give you some back."

"No need. If you're pregnant that's more than enough payment." He rubbed my belly.

"And if I'm not?"

"Then you'll be compensating until you are." I snickered and placed a kiss on his lips.

"You hungry?" He asked after we took one last look at the place. The furniture was being delivered this weekend and I couldn't wait to stay here.

My mom decided to keep the condo and sale the house Mario broke in. She's excited to be somewhere she's not responsible for fixing anything or snow removal. She's far from lazy and has a new man but will tell you in a minute, she ain't built for hard labor unless it's beating someone's ass.

"Yea. I think Paradise sounds good." I told him as he locked the door. I loved that place and his chef always made me the best food. It does help when you're sleeping with the boss tho.

He parked in his spot and walked around the truck to help me out. We were far from dressed up and this place required business or dressy attire. He told me not to worry about it but when we stepped in and everyone looked nice, and I felt uncomfortable. He held my hand and took us to a table in the corner where no one could see anything. I loved this spot and a few times we did inappropriate things here.

"Look who decided to grace us with their presence." Tara sassed and scooted me over.

"Can't you see me and my baby mama tryna have dinner?"

"OH MY GOD! YOU PREGNANT?" She asked excitedly and started feeling my stomach.

"Not yet but it doesn't stop him from trying."

"Hell no and when she gets pregnant, I'm still not pulling out." Tara threw a napkin at him.

"Anyway. My aunt told me about your house being renovated. Don't forget a sister when you throwing BBQ's."

"Never that."

"Damn Tara. It's too early to be inviting yourself to our house." I smiled and didn't even correct him. He considered his place mine so why wouldn't I do the same?

"There you are." We all turned our heads and Monee was standing there outta breath and holding her chest.

"Bitch, if you don't get your dirty ass from over here, I'm gonna beat your face in." I tried to be as calm as possible because if I am expecting, I didn't wanna have a miscarriage from fighting.

"Hold on." This bitch was really testing me, and Remi must've had enough because he pushed Monee back making her hit the floor.

"WAIT! PLEASE. I'M TRYING TO TELL YOU SOMETHING BAD HAPPENED TO YOUR MOTHER." Remi snatched her up off the ground.

"What the fuck you talking about?"

"Babe, she can't speak because you're choking her." I had to make him release her. She hit the floor hard.

"What happened to his mom?" I had to get down to Monee's level because the longer she took to speak, the angrier he was. Tara had a few bouncers come over to hold him.

"I went to the house his brother had and the door was unlocked. His girlfriend was on the ground damn near beat to death. When the EMT's arrived, the cops asked if she knew who did it and she blamed Ivan."

"BITCH YOU SAID MY MOTHER." Remi shouted.

"I rode by his mother's place and there were cops and ambulances there too." Just as she finished telling me, Remi's phone rang and so did Tara's.

"WHAT? WHERE ARE YOU?" I stood in front of Remi.

"Let's go."

"Is she ok?" I asked grabbing my things and running behind her.

"I don't know. My father said she's at the hospital and they don't know if she's going to make it." I saw a few tears falling down his face and snatched the keys out his hand.

"I'll drive." He jumped in the passenger side and we heard the back door open. Tara hopped in the back seat.

"She's gonna be ok Remi." Tara said rubbing his shoulders. I remained quiet because I didn't know what to say.

I grabbed his hand and held the whole way there. I dropped him off at the emergency room door and told them I'd be right in. Remi was very hesitant to allow me outta his sight until Tara reminded him cops were here. He kissed me and said hurry up parking the truck.

I found a parking spot, pulled in and grabbed my purse. As I walked in my mother called. I answered and explained what all Monee told us. My mother couldn't believe it and said she was on her way. After she told me the truth about my father, I introduced her, and Remi and they got along great.

My foot was at the threshold of the door when someone yanked me back and put their hand over my mouth. I started kicking and tried to bite whoever it was.

"It took me forever to get you." I froze.

The person whispering in my ear was the same one who entered my hospital room. He had the familiar smell of liquor and even though he spoke softly, I knew it was him. The tears flowed instantly and even though I could see Remi and his family through the glass, none of them were facing my direction.

"Yo, what you doing?" I heard Mario's voice and did everything I could to break free. This person had a death grip on me. What is he doing here anyway?

"Let her go." Mario ran up and someone came out the shadows and dug a knife in his back.

"AHHHH." He shouted and fell to the ground.

"Help me get her in the van before they notice." All the muffled screaming, kicking and scratching did nothing to help set me free.

BOOM! They tossed me in the van, and I felt a blow to my back. It was so hard, I had to be paralyzed.

"What the fuck? A baseball bat?" The person pulled whoever was with him to the side.

"Yup. Her head is next." This is not how I expected to die.

Cat

"Are you sure this is the house she picked?" I asked my mom.

Ivy finally picked a date she wanted to get married on and one of her gifts was a brand-new house. She loved the other one I purchased but now the memories are too bad. We could stay at my place, but she wanted something bigger due to all the kids she wanted. It's funny because men are usually the ones who want all the bad ass boys running around.

"I'm positive." She had a huge grin on her face.

"Ok. We'll take it." I told the realtor. Now she had a huge grin on her face, and she should. Not only am I paying cash for this spot, her cut is gonna be nice.

The house sat on three acres, had six bedrooms, a basketball court out back, a pool, three car garage and it was fenced in the front and back. Ivy always mentioned tryna learn how to plant flowers and shit. This place is huge so she can plant every tree or flower in the world.

"She's going to be so happy." I filled out all the paperwork and the lady said she'll contact me with a closing date.

"Now let's get her new car."

"Ma, she just got a brand new one last year."

"Exactly! Last year. If you're gonna upgrade, you may as well go all out." I shook my head because she doing the most.

We drove to the Mercedes lot and just like I expected, the sales people rushed over. My mother told them to back up and if we needed them, she'd say something. I couldn't do shit but laugh because they all seemed shocked a woman pushed them away.

"Hey sexy." I answered for Ivy.

"Soooooo I was thinking that next week is a good time to set up a prenatal appointment. I mean we shouldn't wait to..."

"WHAT?" I stopped walking.

"You did it baby."

"Did what?" I knew what she was talking about but wanted to hear her say it.

"We're having a baby." The shit had me smiling from ear to ear.

I wanted her to have my child since the first time we slept together. I understood why she decided to wait and honestly after the things we've been through I'm glad we did. I can't begin to think about what would've happened if our kid was at the house when Wendy and her cousin attacked. The shit makes me mad each time I think about it.

"Are you happy?" Ivy asked and I couldn't stop smiling.

"This is it." My mother spoke softly and pointed to a silver 2019 Mercedes GLC truck.

"Hell yea I'm happy. You know I've been tryna get you pregnant forever." She laughed in the phone.

"Hurry home so I can thank you."

"A'ight but it's gonna have to wait because your mother in law said she staying over."

"It's ok. We got all night."

BEEP! I took the phone from my ear to see who was calling.

"I'll see you when I get there. Remi on the other line."

"Ok tell him to have Naima call me. I've been tryna reach her."

"A'ight."

"Yo!" I clicked over.

"Bro I need you at the hospital." I don't know why but my heart started beating fast.

"You good?"

"Something happened to ma and I can't find Naima. One minute she was parking the truck and the next she went missing. Shit is all fucked up."

"I'll be right there." I hung up and told my mother we'd have to come another day.

"What's going on?"

"I don't know. Remi called and some shit went down with his mom. He can't find Naima and she went there with him." She gasped.

"We should pick Ivy up."

"Nah because she'll worry, and I can't have her losing my baby."

"SHE'S PREGNANT? OH MY GOD!" She was jumping up and down in the seat.

"Calm down ma. We can't go inside being happy when they're going through something."

"Ok. Ok. I hope both of them are ok." It took twenty minutes to get there. My phone rang and it was Ivy again. I wonder if Remi contacted her too.

"Cat, I need you." I stopped walking in the middle of the parking lot.

"What's wrong? Are you ok?" Her voice was trembling, and I could tell she was most likely shaking.

"Baby, they're taking me to jail for murder."

"For what? I know it's not Wendy?" I know damn well we did a good job covering our tracks for her.

"No, it's not for her or the cousin." She whispered as low as she could.

"Then what the fuck they taking you to jail for?"

"Remi's mother. They're saying its attempted murder now but if she dies, its first degree." All the air left my body. This couldn't be happening.

"Ma'am that's enough time. You have the right to remain silent..." I heard an officer in the background right before the phone went dead.

Remi

"Tell me Naima is outside." I rushed over to Cat's mom. She seemed to be shaken up and her eyes were watery.

"Where's Cat?" I peeked around her in search of my boy.

"Remi, Ivy called when we pulled in and said she was being arrested." She placed her hand on the side of my face.

"Arrested? For what?" She swallowed hard.

"For whatever happened to your mom."

"SAY WHAT?" I was about to speak when I noticed Nyeemah's mom step in the hospital. My phone went off at the same time. I spoke and told her to give me a minute.

"Who this?" I never bothered to look at the number because not only was Ivy arrested for my mother, here was Naima's searching the waiting room for her daughter.

"Remington Stevens III." The man speaking my full name on the phone had my attention.

"It's a lot going on tonight, isn't it?" I glanced around the waiting room myself and no one had a phone to their ear.

"Who the fuck is this?"

"Tsk, Tsk, Tsk. Is that the way you speak to the man who holds your future in his hands?" I chuckled.

"This must be Julio." Now it was his turn to laugh.

"Correct."

"What you want and how the fuck you holding my future in your hands?"

"It seems Naima is missing; your mother suffered some pain this evening and your brother is beating up old girlfriends of yours. The way I see it is, you can't possibly run businesses when your name is attached to scandals."

"Nigga shut the fuck up. What you calling me for?" I wasn't about to go back and forth with this nigga.

"All I want is what's been taking from me years ago." He said smugly in the phone.

"You watching my girl over a damn ring?"

"Ahh. So you know what I want? Your father must've filled you in."

"Look. This shit is childish as fuck right now. We'll deal with you another time." I hung up on him and walked over to my pops who looked stressed out.

"I've been in jail for years Remi and all I thought about the entire time is coming home to my family. I can't lose my wife, son." It's like the entire emergency room went silent.

"Pops she's not gonna die."

"You didn't see her. Blood was everywhere and she was barely breathing."

"How did you know?" I asked because my father was at my office counting money for me. I've been running around doing other things and with the accountant gone, I had to make sure my money was on point until I found another one.

"I don't know how she did it, but your mom called me and said to hurry home. I didn't even bother asking what happened and called the cops myself. I flew home and when I got there the cops and ambulance were pulling up at the same time."

"Was anyone there with her?" I wanted to know if a neighbor saw what happened or if they saw Ivy leaving.

"No one was with her and that's what's fucking me up. She laid there dying and I don't even know if she had any idea I was there. Son she was…" He stopped speaking and wiped his eyes.

"Have you looked at the cameras in the house yet?" He shook his head no.

"I can't right now. I don't wanna see what went down until I know she's ok." I sat next to him.

"The nigga called requesting his ring." My father looked at me. I had to change the subject because he was making me more upset.

"Talking about he knows everything going on within the family."

"I'm not surprised." I blew my breath and sat back. I had to tell him about my girl.

"Naima's missing and they've arrested Ivy for ma."

"What?" My phone rang again. This time I looked hoping it was Naima, but the number was blocked.

"Now what?" I knew it was Julio again by the voice. He really had too much time on his hands.

"You should go to the window."

"Didn't I tell you I'm not playing these games."

"Well, I guess you're not tryna save Naima after all." I stood up quick.

"Go to the window." I ran over in hopes to see her.

"That black van has her inside." I went to the door.

"Tell her mother who's standing directly next to you I'm not playing and if the ring isn't returned, she will regret it." I repeated his statement. She asked for the phone and I don't know what they spoke about but she was cursing him out.

"Fuck this." I ran out the door.

BOOM! The van exploded in front of me. My ears were ringing as I hit the ground, but that screeching scream could be heard miles away.

"NOOOOOO!"

At the Hospital…

Ivan

"Give me the got damn bat." I snatched it outta Monee's hand before she could hit her again.

I told the bitch to help me kidnap Naima and here she is tryna kill her with a baseball bat. She's been working with me for a while now and of course we fucked in the process. She knows damn well killing ain't in her blood.

After seeing Naima whoop her ass outside the restaurant, I guess having her at a disadvantage is the only way she'd beat her and I couldn't disagree.

"Let me kill her Ivan. I hate this bitch." I pushed her toward the passenger side of the van and made her get in.

"You out here throwing a fucking tantrum and we need to get outta here." I slammed the door and jumped in the driver side.

"I'm saying Ivan. It's the only way to get Remi away from her." This bitch wanted my brother bad as hell.

She was dick whipped or something over Remi. Don't ask me why when she constantly complained about how he spoke to her. The bitch will fuck anyone and damn sure can't suck dick and from what Nelly said, my dick is little so it's no reason Monee be gagging. It's not like I'm hitting her tonsils or maybe I am. Whatever the case, she needs acid reflux pills for dick or something.

"Stop worrying about that nigga." She turned her head and stared out the window. If the bitch wanted to help me spend this money she better get on board and stop worrying about Remi. Shit, as we can all tell, he ready to go to war over his bitch.

After I whooped Nelly's ass for the disrespectful shit she said to me, I went and beat up my mother. I didn't mean to but I snapped when she told me to leave. Like how she making me go when she invited me to eat? Then gonna get mad because I don't wanna speak as I'm chewing. I bet she won't do that again; not as if she can now anyway.

Once I handled her and took the money, I hit Monee up because she was in on me getting Remi in a compromising position at Club Turquoise. I had her show up at the grand opening, which by the way was fun until the bitch smacked me. Why she put hands on me knowing I'd hit her back was stupid on her part? I'm more mad my brother took her side without even tryna listen to my story. Granted she didn't lie but so what? What if she did? He automatically believed her.

In any case, after I did that to my mother, I had Monee go to each of Remi's businesses searching for him. He wasn't at any of them at first, but she found him at the new restaurant. She pretended to be upset about my mother and made up a good ass story. Who knew Naima would be an easy target? I thought she'd get to the hospital and he'd have a tight grip on her. But no, he let her park the car and I snatched her up on the way in. Unfortunately, some dude tried to save her and Monee stabbed him. For someone who was scared in the beginning to go against Remi, it sure doesn't seem like it now.

Right after we abducted Naima, I sent Monee's brother on a goose chase to Cat's house. I told him he had a safe and it was easy to get the money out of it because he doesn't keep it locked. I called the cops and told them the person responsible for my mother was Ivy Blackmon and they could find her at his house. I gave the address and told them I was driving by and saw her run out the house, in which I followed.

I expected Monee's brother to kill Ivy so she wouldn't be able to defend herself against the claim of murdering my mother. Who knew she had a gun in the house? It didn't stop the cops from arresting Ivy tho. They had her down at the station for hours Monee told me. Yea, she was the lookout while I stayed with Naima thinking of a plan.

****

"Where am I?" I turned and stared at Naima lying on the couch in Monee's house. I would've left town, but I'm not finished handling my family.

"It's about time you woke up." I walked over and stood in front of her. She was a beautiful woman and I could see why my brother fell for her. Shit, I could've had her if she wasn't a bitch in the beginning.

"Ivan? What the hell?" She attempted to move but you could tell by her facial expression she was in pain.

"We meet again sexy."

"Fuck you."

WHAP! I backhanded her so hard she fell off the couch.

"No one is here to help you this time." I lifted her by the head and smacked her over and over.

"Please stop." She begged and pleaded until I let go. One of her eyes was closed shut and her nose bled.

"Dammit! I got some of your blood on me." I tossed her head on the floor and stepped over her to clean my hands in the kitchen sink. I could hear her crying and shouting for help. All she did is enrage me more because Monee lived in an apartment so it's no telling who could hear.

"Shut the fuck up before I find something to tape your mouth with." The room got quiet.

"What's going on?" Monee asked and dropped her keys on the kitchen counter.

"Monee? You too?" Naima questioned. This dumb bitch kicked her in the head and was about to stomp on her face.

"Calm the hell down. You know like I do if she dies, he'll come looking for you too." Monee was playing the hell outta this tough role.

"That's why I told you to let me kill her with the bat. They don't know who took her so we would've gotten away with it." I shook my head.

"Help me get her in the bed." I lifted her arm to stand.

"You ain't fucking her in my room." I yoked her up by the shirt.

"Bitch are you crazy? I may have slapped her around a few times here and there but I ain't no fucking rapist." I tossed Monee on the ground. Say what you want but I would never force a woman to sleep with me.

"Then why you want her in there?"

"Duhhhh. I'm gonna make it look like we slept together. That way Remi won't assume Naima's kidnapped and think she left willingly." An evil grin came across her face.

The two of us helped Naima off the floor, dragged her up the steps and threw her in the bed. I forced her to remove her shirt and bra. I'm not gonna lie, my dick grew at the sight. She tried to cover herself, but I moved her hands out the way.

I took my shirt off, laid her down with me on top and started kissing her neck. Monee instantly picked up her phone to snap pictures. I told her to take as many as possible without the fucked up eye. With Naima fighting, we had to get the right one to send Remi and boy did we get one.

It was perfect too. My mouth was on hers and our tongues were touching until she bit down and I punched her in the face, knocking her out. Monee thought it was the funniest thing ever.

I eventually got up, snatched Monee and fucked her on the couch. Shit, lying on top of Naima turned me on so much I needed a release. It's unfortunate the bitch was on my mind the whole time but like I said, I'm not raping nobody.

"Now what?" Monee asked sitting next to me on the couch.

"Go down to the hospital and show Remi. Make sure you pay attention to his expression and give me details on how he took it." She nodded. I went upstairs to shower and take it down for the night. I couldn't wait for her to tell me what happened.

Remi

The explosion not only caught me off guard but had me laid the fuck out. I couldn't move and the ringing along with the screaming wouldn't go away. It's like that annoying noise coming from an alarm; only it was a bomb. A bomb that most likely shook the ground, blasted out windows and caused other vehicles to catch on fire. How did he pull this shit off?

Each second passing, people were running around me and cops were now surrounding the area. All I could think about is Julio killing Naima and possibly our baby if she were pregnant. Was her body in the truck or did she make it out? It never hurt to keep positives thoughts when bad things happen.

"Sir, can you hear me?" A man in a white coat stood over me. He was yelling for someone to bring a few men out and a stretcher.

"Sir, you're gonna be ok." The guy said.

"What the hell is going on?" My father's voice boomed in the parking lot.

"Where's my son?" I tried to speak but it was no use. It hurt to take breaths and the ringing wouldn't stop.

"Shit. Remi are you ok?" My father kneeled down beside me.

"Excuse us sir. We need to slide him on this board and then the stretcher." My pops moved back and watched as they did what was necessary and lifted me up.

"You're gonna be fine son. I'll be right here." He squeezed my hand and inside I could vaguely hear Cat's mom on the phone.

"Oh my God Cat. Get down here. Something bad happened to Remi." Again, it hurt to breathe so I couldn't even tell her I'd be ok.

"Move out the way." The doctors shouted and I heard doors opening.

"He needs a Cat scan and MRI of his entire body. I want a cardiologist and orthopedic down here ASAP." I could see people running around.

"Let's get him done because they're more casualties and possible fatalities. Evidently, the vehicle that blew up caused others to as well and people were either in them or walking in the area." I closed my eyes hoping I'd wake up because the pain I'm feeling had me believing this is it. The doctor spoke a few more times and that's all I remember.

****

"Welcome back Mr. Stevens." The doctor said when my eyes opened. He pulled out the small flashlight and began doing an examination. Thankfully, I could feel all my body parts.

"Is my mother ok? Is my girl here? Where's my pops?" I asked question after question waiting for him to answer at least one.

"Can you excuse us doctor?" I turned my head to see Nyeemah sitting in a chair close to the window. He finished examining me and closed the door on his way out.

"When Naima was born it was the happiest day of my life. She was beautiful and had the loudest scream one could ever hear." I pressed the button for my bed to rise. It felt weird lying flat while she spoke.

"Her father was happier than a pig in shit." She tossed her head back laughing.

"Three years, he had the pleasure of raising his daughter and Naima was his pride and joy. If anyone told you she ate her food with her mouth open he'd call you a liar, even if he saw it with his own eyes."

"Nyeemah." I wanted to ask why she told me all this.

"One night his life was cut shirt over jealousy and a stupid ring. A FUCKING RING REMI!" She banged on the wall.

"Now my daughter is missing all because he refuses to allow a debt that was paid to stay that way. He wants to renege on it over money."

"Missing?" She turned and wiped her face.

"Naima was never in the van Remi."

"WHAT?" I held my stomach. The explosion gave me a concussion, some bruised ribs and a fractured wrist.

"Julio knew you'd run out and expected you to save her. I tried to call you back, but it was too late." Furious can't explain how angry I was. This motherfucker was playing a bunch of games. I can't wait until we get his ass.

"If you died it would be one less person in the way."

"Wait! If the ring is all he wants, then why go after Naima?" She pulled her chair up close to me.

"Oh Remi. You have no idea how the love a man holds for a woman can make you do stupid things."

"Trust me, I know." I pointed to myself.

"No. You were trying to save my daughter; the love of your life. No, it's different." Her head went back and forth.

"Julio wants Naima dead because in his eyes, I wasn't supposed to have a child by another man and since I did, he's going to take her away from me."

"Are you serious?" The fear on her face let me know it's true.

"It's unfortunate he couldn't allow the past to stay there." She started tearing up again after saying it.

"What do you mean?"

"His daughter will receive her demise soon enough and when she dies, it will be up to you to keep Naima safe. He will try even harder afterwards"

"His daughter? How he going after yours when he has one by another I'm assuming?"

"A man's pride always gets in the way of doing the right thing." She stood.

"So you see Remi, the person who has my daughter is not Julio, nor is he working with him. Noooo, this person has been watching her closely."

"Mario?" She gave me a crazy look.

"Mario was attacked outside the hospital trying to save her."

"Say what?" She told me how Mario came to see his father at the hospital because he was hurt at work, when he saw a man covering Naima's mouth. He tried to intervene, and someone dug a knife in his back. His lung collapsed and they had to rush him into surgery. He asked to speak with her afterwards and gave the best description of the guy he could. It's unfortunate the guy had on all black and even a mask.

"I have to get outta here." I lifted the covers and she stopped me.

"You won't be any good going after her while you're hurt."

"I can't have my girl out there missing with no one tryna find her."

"You're not the only one with people Remi." She smiled.

"Her cousins are searching for her now, but I will tell you when they get to Naima, your brother will take his last breath."

"What does Ivan have to do with this?" She grabbed her things and kissed my forehead.

"He's the one who kidnapped Naima outside the hospital last night." She left the room and no matter how many times I called her back, she never returned.

"What you in here yelling about?" Tara stepped in with my aunt and two of my uncles.

"Ivan kidnapped Naima. I have to..."

"We already know. Your father has people on it and so does her family." My uncle said and told me to get back in the bed.

"He's gonna kill her."

"Doubt it. His dumb ass already asked for a ransom assuming we don't know it's him." My uncle Jack laughed as he said it.

"How did y'all find out?"

"Security cameras."

"But Nyeemah's mom said he was covered up."

"She wanted to see where your head was at before mentioning it. She's gonna be fine Remi."

"And my mother? How is she?" Tara and her mom both sat on the side of me.

"Thankfully she's going to live but not without complications."

"What you mean?"

"The person managed to rip her hair out, which made her scalp open and caused a minor infection. Her nose is broke and so are a few of her fingers. One of her ribs are cracked and her lung collapsed. The left eye is swollen and they're waiting for her to wake up to make sure her hearing is intact. Remi whoever did this tried to kill her." I shook my head no. My mother didn't deserve this and whoever did this is going to suffer.

"Did pops watch the video yet?"

"He hasn't left your moms side." I nodded because if I weren't in here and Naima was ok, I wouldn't have left her either.

"Remi, Ivy didn't do it and..." I cut Tara off.

"I know she had nothing to do with it just like all of you. My question is, who set her up and why?" No one said a word. Someone wanted all of us to suffer and I'll be damned if they're aren't doing a good job at it.

Cat

"Yea ma?" I answered the phone on the first ring. I know she was calling to find out about Ivy.

"Cat, something bad happened to Remi." I slammed on my brakes.

"Say what?" She proceeded to tell me how there was an explosion and Remi was caught in it somehow and they rushed him in the back.

"FUCK!" I banged on the steering wheel a few times. Why is all this shit happening to us?

"Ma, tell him I'll be there as soon as I get Ivy out." She told me ok and hung the phone up. This entire situation had to be set up by Julio. Its no other person who could possibly pull this type of shit off. I parked in front of the police station, ran inside and demanded answers.

"Sir, I understand your frustration, but Ms. Blackmon has been arrested for the attempted murder of Mrs. Stevens." The captain at the police department told me.

"Exactly but why? Huh? Explain to me how someone broke into my house, assaulted her and you take her out in handcuffs for a crime committed on the other side of town because I'm confused as fuck?" I argued with my lawyer sitting next to me.

When Ivy called, I had my mom go check on Remi's mother at the hospital while I rushed down to the station. This was before I found out he was hurt too. My girl calls me with this shit about being arrested and we still don't know why she's really here.

I don't know if I was more concerned with her health or the fact someone broke in my house. I had alarms and they didn't go off on my phone. I only found out someone broke in because of the video I pulled up on the app.

Ivy was sitting in the living room and someone rang the doorbell. She went to answer it and the person pushed her out the way. He ransacked the house looking for who knows what. I watched Ivy go in her purse, pull out the gun I purchased since the shit with Wendy and shoot him.

Afterwards, she picked the phone up and contacted the police. What I didn't understand is how they even considered her a suspect in what happened to Remi's mom when she was protecting herself at home?

"If you would calm down, I'll be happy to explain." The captain tried to keep me calm but nothing he said made sense.

"Explain after my fiancé is out." I stood and my lawyer told him Ivy should've been released by now.

"She's getting out on her own recognizance, but she cannot leave the state or..."

"Man shut the fuck up." I swung the door open and Ivy limped straight to me. Her foot was still fucked up but she refused to use the crutches. She said her underarms were sore.

"Baby why are they saying I hurt Remi's mom?" She cried in my arms. I lifted her up in my arms and carried her out. She rested her head on my neck and held me tight.

"I'll call you tomorrow." My lawyer said and I placed Ivy in the car.

"Where's Naima?" I had no knowledge pf what was going on at the hospital and didn't wanna give her the wrong information.

"Let me get you home." I closed the door and drove off in silence. I heard her sniffling the whole way.

"You're not going to jail." I told Ivy when I carried her in the house.

"Cat, they're saying I hurt his mom and..."

"And we all know it's not true. You were here protecting yourself at the same time his mom was attacked. It doesn't make sense because you couldn't be in two places at once. What I'm wrecking my brain to find out is, who set you up and is the break in connected?"

"I don't know but can we stay at a hotel?" I glanced around the room and noticed blood on the floor. The guy didn't die but she definitely got his ass. I asked the captain where he was and he told me at the hospital. Once I get her situated, I'm going there to question him right after I see Remi and his mom.

I called my mother back while we grabbed some stuff and she told me all hell broke loose in the hospital. She also said his mom is messed up pretty bad and it was touch and go for a few hours. The explosion from the Julio dude surprised me the most. I also know if he did murder Naima, Remi is gonna lose it.

****

"How's she doing?" I asked big Remi. He stood outside the hospital room in ICU. Its been two days since everything happened and I'm just making it up here. Ivy was scared and didn't want me to leave her. I spoke to my boy on the phone a few times, but the conversations were short due to the pain he was in.

"Stable right now. Cat, when I find out who did this…" I hugged him because at the end of the day, Remi's mom has been a part of my life growing up too.

Even though he was incarcerated, I visited with big Remi quite a bit and considered both of them my second parents. I can't imagine what he's going through.

"You want me to go by the house and check the cameras when I leave?" I asked because he hasn't moved and all of us wanna know who did this.

"My brother went to get it."

"I told you to get the alarm with the app that comes to your phone." Remi and I kept telling him the new alarms were better because you had access at all times.

"You know I'm still getting used to being home. Plus, she already had the security system set up. I'm gonna get that one when we get outta here."

"A'ight. What's up tho? Does anyone have any idea who could've done it?" He looked at me.

"They tryna get Ivy for it but we know that's bullshit." I felt relieved he didn't even question me about them accusing her.

"Where's Naima? Ivy keeps asking for her." He ran his hand down his face. Each time my girl asked, I redirected the question to something else. Remi told me she was missing on the phone yesterday, but I figured she was back by now.

"Ivan kidnapped her outside the hospital."

"Come again."

"Yea and Remi just found out."

"How the fuck he do that?" I was confused. Ivan is a bitch. I'm amazed he pulled it off.

"Naima went to park his truck while him and Tara ran in. He must've known she'd come here and..." He stopped as if something went off in his head.

"Hold up." He started pacing.

"How the fuck did Ivan know to come here for her? No one got the chance to call him." His facial expression changed, and I swear, I'd be scared if I didn't know who he was mad at.

"Yo, you're not thinking what I'm thinking."

"If that nigga did this to my wife; his mother, ain't nothing stopping me from killing him."

"Ivan crazy but he ain't that crazy." I tried to give him the benefit of the doubt.

"How else can he explain being here when no one called him? Think about it. Ivan was pissed my wife punched him in the face and kicked him out. He was popping mad shit and even though I told her not to contact his bitch ass, she didn't like the atmosphere of them not speaking. What if she called him to talk and he came over and did this?"

"I don't even know what to say because it sounds suspect as fuck. Does anyone know where he is?"

"Everybody searching for him. FUCK! I'm gonna snap his body in half if this is his doing." The machines started beeping inside the room.

We both ran in and Remi's mom eyes were opened. This big ass man broke down. I've seen men cry on TV and at funerals and shit but never like this. He was letting the tears roll and kept telling her nothing else was going to happen.

"I'm ok Remington." She told him after the doctors checked. She rubbed the top of his head.

"Where is Remi?" She spoke quietly.

"There was an accident outside the hospital and…" She immediately started crying.

"Please don't tell me Ivan got to him too."

"WHAT?" Remington stood up ready to fight.

"I should've listened to you and none of this would've happened." She cried harder.

"All of this is because of him." She pointed to her body.

"I called him over to talk and he went crazy. He backhanded me first and then grabbed my leg. He took the money out the safe. I should've listened." Remington tried to leave the room, but his brothers came just in time.

"He wanted me to die so he could get my insurance policy. Remington what happened to him? Why is he like this?" Big Remi hugged her, and I could see him fighting with himself about leaving.

"He's jealous of his brother and thinks you cater to him." I told her and they all shook their heads.

Ivan has been this way ever since Remi started making money. Remi offered him to work alongside of us, but he was always to busy. He was busy alright. Busy spending the money and sitting on his lazy ass.

"I tried to tell him otherwise, but he lost it. I'm sorry babe." She had him sit down next to her.

"Umm, I'm gonna let Remi know you're awake." I told her and went towards the door.

"Please don't tell him."

"Huh?" I questioned because its no way in hell I'm keeping it a secret.

"He's gonna kill Ivan."

"He deserves to die after what he did. You almost died." His father was pissed off.

"I don't want to bury my son."

"Too got damn bad." Remi's pops said with finality and no one said a word. I kissed her cheek and excused myself from the room. Remington came out behind me.

"Tell Remi. We need to have all eyes searching for that nigga."

"You already know." He gave me a hug and asked me to let Remi know he'll be there." I pressed the elevator and went up to his floor. When I stepped in his room, I was shocked to see her there on his bed.

Remi

"Oh my God Remi, are you ok?" Monee barged in my room yelling like a fool. The last time I saw her, I almost put a bullet in her side. Now she's here pretending to care about me. That's how you can tell she's up to no good and I'm sure it'll show soon.

"What you doing here Monee?" I continued eating the nasty ass jello the hospital offered. I was waiting on Cat to get up here because I damn sure was asking him to get me some outside food.

"Word is out you almost died, and I had to check on you." I looked over at her.

"How is that?"

"It's all over the news Remi and they said your name."

"Hmph." I didn't say anything and allowed her to sit there going on and on about some BS.

"Oh, this was on your brothers page on FB." She passed me her phone and showed me a photo where Ivan lay on top of my girl bare chested. I knew the real reason she's here would come out soon and here it is.

"Oh, so he sleeping with her now?"

"That's what I said. Does he wanna be you?" She asked with a straight face.

"Who knows? You seen him?" I pried hoping she'd give me information on his whereabouts. I'm gonna kill him for touching Naima because I told him before to stay away. It's obvious he doesn't listen and loves testing me. This will be the last time.

"No." I smirked because the bitch is stupid.

"You good bro?" Cat asked walking in staring at Monee.

"I'm good. Is Ivy still locked up for doing that shit to my mom?" I gave him a look and luckily, he caught on.

"Yea. They won't let me get her out." He stood against the wall on the side of me.

"Well she shouldn't be allowed out if it happened. What the fuck was she thinking?" Monee didn't say a word and pecked away on her phone.

"A'ight thanks for stopping by." She glanced up from her phone and appeared to be offended.

"You want me to go?"

"Yea bitch. It's clear as day we need to discuss what his girl did." She pouted but took her ass outta here.

"Pass me my phone." Cat handed it to me and I called my pops.

"What's wrong?"

"I need you to contact Naima's people and tell them Ivan has her at Monee's house. This is her address." I read it off and put the phone down.

The hospital made me stay a few days due to the concussion and cracked ribs. They wanted to monitor me, otherwise I would've already been kicking down the bitch door.

"How you know she there?"

"I've been to Monee's house and the picture she had, showed her bedroom set and those hello kitty curtains."

"Hello Kitty? Ain't she too old for that?"

"Exactly. Its all good though because it showed me, she's been working with him." He finally took a seat next to me and I couldn't help but wonder if my pops got in touch with Naima's cousins. I didn't have to wait long because he sent me a message saying they were on their way to get her. I felt a little relieved but aggravated because I couldn't be there.

"They're gonna get her bro." Cat reassured me. I hope they do before he attempts to move her. Ain't no telling what Ivan got going on in his head.

"What's going on with Ivy?" He started explaining how someone broke in the house, she shot him, and the cops came accusing her of what went down with my mom. The shit is crazy because you can't be in two places at one time.

"Hey." My pops strolled in with his hands in his pockets. One of my uncles came in behind him.

"How's ma?"

"She's good considering."

"Considering what?" All three of them looked at me. I stared over at Cat who had a sad look on his face. Did he know what my father was about to say?

"Considering Ivan is the person who attacked her."

"Come again because I know damn well you didn't just say my brother did this to my mother."

"Remi, she told us when her eyes opened but she doesn't want anyone to go after him."

"That's too fucking bad. I'm killing his ass." I tossed the covers off my legs and attempted to get up but with the way my ribs felt, I wasn't going anywhere.

"Naima's people are on their way to Monee's crib. I told them to kill him on sight. That way it won't be either of us who did it."

"This is fucking crazy. Did she say why he beat her?" He ran his hand down his face and my uncle shook his head.

"What did I tell you a while back about Ivan?"

"I don't know pops. We discussed a lot." We did and at the moment I really had no time for guessing games.

"I told you he was jealous, and Cat told you he's tryna sabotage anything you have."

"Ok." I said.

"Your brother is the true definition of a hater. He wants what you have and emptied the safe in our room."

"WHAT?" I shouted. I always put money in the safe just to make sure if my mother needed money and I was outta the country or something, she'd have it.

I would've done the same for Ivan, but he was careless with his money, which is why I had an accountant. That got me nowhere though because his dumb ass let Ivan do whatever; including getting a condo for some bitch.

"He's expecting her to die so he can get her insurance policy." I couldn't believe the extent of bullshit my brother was going through to destroy our family. He had everything he could possibly want and it still wasn't enough.

"Take me to see ma." He nodded and walked out to have a nurse bring in a wheelchair.

When we got down there the nurse had us wait because my mom wanted to get washed up. After she finished and we went in, I had to check myself from crying like a baby. My mother was fucked up and I hated no one could save her at the time.

"Remi. Thank God you're ok. Did they get Naima yet and where's Ivy?"

"Not yet and Ivy is at a hotel. She's scared someone's after her." I said and asked everyone to give us a minute.

Once the door closed, I stared at her. The monitors on her chest, bandage on her head, the different braces and her overall appearance fucked me up. My mother is beautiful and always happy. To see her sad and hurt, did something to me because I wasn't there to save her. What if she died?

"I'm ok son." She rubbed the top of my head.

"You can't save him anymore." I told her and meant exactly what I said. No mother wants to bury their child but it's a no brainer now.

"I know."

"Ma, just know if it were another way to get rid of him without doing the inevitable, I would."

"The sad thing about your brother is he didn't want to do better. He never wanted to work and expected handouts every time." I glanced up at her.

"We both enabled him Remi whether you see it that way or not." I nodded.

"It doesn't mean he should've done this, tried to destroy your businesses or take your girl." I sucked my teeth and she lifted my face.

"I'm talking about Naima. Remi that woman loves the ground you walk on and Ivan knows it. He thought he'd be able to persuade her to be with him the way Nelly was. When she didn't and he noticed the love she held for you, he said anything to make her leave and she still wouldn't."

"Who would've ever thought my brother would be this jealous of me?" I shook my head because its all I could do.

"There's always one in the family. It's unfortunate your brother is the one." She was staring at the television.

"How will you do it?"

"I don't know ma. I wanna torture him after seeing you and hearing he kidnapped Naima, but then I wanna get it over and done with because at the end of the day, he's still my brother."

"I don't want your father doing it because he just gotta outta jail. He'll be careless and I don't want him or you getting locked up."

"I'll try and beat him to it but again, you know how he is over you." She smiled.

"I love you Remi and I'm sorry your brother is hateful." I stood and winced in pain.

"Ma, don't apologize for his actions. He's a grown ass man and he knows the consequences." I hugged her and she started to cry.

I know she's going through something but when your own child is trying to kill you, there's no other choice.

"I don't want my son to die but if he has to, I'd rather know it was done by you."

"Ma, stop thinking about it."

"I'll try." I moved away and she wiped her eyes.

"Stop making my wife cry." My pops barked coming in the room with Cat and my uncle.

"Remington, I've come to grips with it but I want Remi doing it." He looked at me.

"You know I wanted to do it for all the shit in the past. He needs me to snap his got damn neck or…" My mom put her hand up when he started saying and demonstrating the things he wanted to do.

"I don't want my child to die Remington. I also know if I ask you not to, one of you will make it look like an accident anyway." All of us smirked.

"But I don't want to hear you discussing it either. I'm already hurting knowing its going to be done." She started crying again.

"Ma, I'm going back to my room." I kissed her cheek and Cat pushed me in the chair to my room.

"She's gonna take it hard when the time comes." Cat said an I agreed. No parent wants to hear their child will be killed and to know your other child is the one who's gonna do it, has to be hard.

Cat and I spoke a little longer and he told me he'd come back up tomorrow. I laid there hoping they got to Naima in time and how I'm gonna take my brother's life.

Naima

"How did it go? Did he believe you?" I heard Ivan asking Monee. I've been here two maybe three days and I haven't had so much as a shower, food or contact with anyone besides them. I don't expect either of them to do me any favors, but they can at least give me bread and water.

"I showed him the pictures and he asked if Naima was with you now?" Monee teased.

"What? No. No. No." I was devastated listening to them discuss how they portrayed me and Ivan as a couple. After what Nelly did when they were younger, I didn't want Remi to believe I'd do him the same.

"Awwww. What's the matter? Scared your precious Remi will leave you alone?" Ivan joked.

"Why are you doing this?"

"Because I can bitch." He spat and turned to Monee.

"He don't want your fishy ass when he can have all this?" She walked in front of me.

"Yea ok. He'll want the woman who can't take dick or suck it." She stopped and stared. Remi shouted it out when he pulled the gun on her at the restaurant. Once he and I made up, I asked him what he meant by it.

"Oh, you think you're better than me?"

"No I don't. I'm just..." This bitch kicked me on the side so hard I fell over.

"Yea. I don't see you saying shit now." I stared at this trick outta the one eye I could see, and Ivan stood there shaking his head.

"You doing too much. Move." He pushed her out the way, helped me up and sat me on the couch.

"How you expect us to get any money in the ransom if you kill her beforehand?" Ivan barked and she followed him in the other room.

"Fuck her. Let's kill her and pretend she's still alive."

"Dummy, he'll want to see her on FaceTime or something."

"True." *She is really dumb.*

"I'll be back." Ivan told her and headed to the door.

"Where you going?"

"To the store. I have to get stuff to clean her up with." He peeked out the window and looked both ways before leaving me with the idiot.

"What did he see in you?" She turned her face up.

"All women who lose the man they want ask the same question. Why don't you ask him?" She stormed off in the other room. I tried to run out but the pain in my side made me sit right where I was.

BOOM! I jumped when the door flew off the hinges.

"Ritchie?" I cried looking at my cousin with a big ass gun in his hand.

"FUCK! Get her outta here." My other cousin Terry picked me up off the couch.

"What the fuck you in here doing bitch?" I turned my head to Monee and laughed. The heffa peed on herself.

"Hello Monee." Ritchie spoke as if he knew her.

"This was all her idea. She wanted us to kidnap her and make everyone think she was abducted."

"She wanted you to beat her up like that too, right?" Ritchie asked moving closer to her. Monee was now pressed against the wall scared to death.

"Please don't kill me." She cried.

"Take her to the hospital." Terry rushed me down the steps and gently laid me on the back seat.

"You're gonna be ok Naima." Terry said closing the driver's side door.

"Yea. I have her. A'ight." I heard my cousin on the phone and asked who he was talking to.

"Big Remi. He said your man is waiting for you." I smiled and closed my eyes. I'll see Remi shortly. At least I know I'm safe.

****

"How you feeling?" I woke up in the hospital with Remi lying next to me. I hugged him tight.

"I thought he was going to kill me." I cried on his shoulder.

"He won't touch you again." He ran his hand down my face.

"I missed you."

"I missed you too Naima."

"What happened to you?" He had a bandage or something around his waist and a brace on his wrist.

"Julio called and claimed to have you in a van. I ran out to save you and it exploded." I gasped.

"He's really tryna get the ring back but your mother hit me up on some real shit."

"What she say?"

"Julio wants you dead because you're not his." I tensed up when he said it. It only clarified two people wanting me dead.

"Say what?"

"He felt your mother should've never had kids by anyone but him. Therefore; he wants you gone."

"I don't even know the man."

"You don't have to. He knows who you are and we have to get him first, which will happen soon."

"How soon?"

"When all of us get outta here and I deal with Ivan." I stared at him.

"It's a lot going on and right now I don't wanna talk about it." I nodded.

"I just wanna enjoy my girl and my mother being safe." I placed my arm on his stomach and laid on his chest the best I could without hurting him.

"Where's Ivy?" I asked because I'm shocked she isn't up here.

"At a hotel. She'll be here tomorrow."

"I'm sorry all this is happening to us." I lifted my head to kiss him.

"When it comes to Ivan, it was gonna happen whether you were around her not. His jealousy got so bad he became obsessed with hurting me." I shook my head.

"When we're both better, I'll try to relax you." He smirked.

"I'll be right here waiting." I let my hand go under the covers and in his shorts. The least I can do is give him a hand job.

"Mmm." He silently moaned and slipped his tongue in my mouth. My hand went faster, and he grew harder.

"Sssss." His body stiffened.

"You ok? You want me to stop?" I wasn't sure if his stomach hurt.

"No keep going. I'm about to... oh shit..." He squeezed me tight and came on my hand.

"I needed that."

"I'm glad I could give it to you." I got out the bed slow and realized the IV was in my other arm. I moved the bag off the pole and took it in the bathroom with me. I had to wash my hands and bring him a washcloth.

"You're fine Naima." I didn't realize I was crying in the mirror until he walked in. I knew my eye was swollen but the bruises on my face and body were horrific.

"Why would they do this to me?" He turned me around and hugged me.

"Monee is gone and once we find Ivan, he will be too."

"Find him?"

"He was gone when they got you." How the hell was he gone, and he left a minute or two before they kicked the door down? I guess he ran. I felt my gown and body being lifted, wrapped my legs around his waist and my arms on his neck.

"They're all gonna die." I nodded. He rubbed the tip of his dick up and down my pussy that was soaking wet from listening to him moan a short time ago and put him in.

"Sssss." It felt so good and the two of us engaged in pleasing one another for as long as our body would let us. We had no business having sex. I mean between the both of us, our bodies were beat up and the bathroom was tight, but we got it done.

"Feel better?" Remi asked opening the door. We just finished washing up.

"I do now. Thanks babe." I kissed his lips and walked ahead of him. I was really in love with this man and I hoped he felt the same.

Ivan

"You got some nerve showing up here after what you did." Nelly said when I walked in her sister's house. I found out she was here because her mother told me in the store. Evidently, she never mentioned who attacked her. She asked me to come see her and try to make her talk.

"You ain't dead though so why you mad?" She rolled her eyes.

"The only reason I didn't tell on you is because I need my things out the house and you're gonna pay me to keep quiet."

"I'm not paying you shit and since you're aware of the things I'm capable of, threatening me should never leave your mouth." I sat on the bed next to her and stared.

Nelly is a pretty woman but she fucked up by sleeping with me for all the wrongs reasons. Granted, she could've continued without telling me her true intentions, but she wanted to be tough and look where it got her. Some broken ribs, a black eye and who knows what else. Then she wants to sit here and threaten me.

"I came up with a plan to kill Remi." She snapped her neck to look at me.

"What? I'm saying he took the money I had in the duffle bag and won't give it back." I was referring to the money out the safe I removed from my mothers' house.

The day I walked out Monee's house, I used the rent a car to run down to the pharmacy and grab band aids, along with other stuff to clean Naima up. I could care less about the bitch, but I do know, if my brother fights to get her back, he'll wanna see her. If by some chance she looks fucked up, he'll have a fit and won't give me shit.

Monee's ass knew just like I did Naima would rock her had she not been outta commission. I never understood why women attack another when the person can't fight back, but then again, I do it too. The feeling of knowing you're gonna win is fun.

Anyway, I forgot my wallet and the duffle bag full of money and turned around to get it. I didn't trust Monee and wanted to keep the money with me any time I left. Unfortunately, just that fast, I saw men running in Monee's spot and knew off the bat, they weren't there for her; especially with the door kicked off the hinges. I watched from a distance as they carried Naima out and placed her in a car. Monee came out kicking and screaming but nothing bothered them, and the sad part is, I knew she wasn't gonna make it past tonight.

I parked a few streets over for hours waiting for them to leave and when they did, I continued waiting thinking they'd return. Eventually, I fell asleep in the car and when I woke up, I walked to Monee's house. I peeked around before going to the door and ran in, hoping and praying no one found the bag.

Unfortunately, the money was gone and I had nowhere to go. I did the only thing I could think of and went to Remi's place. I know he most likely had a safe and if not, he always kept money lying around.

Sadly, he had the locks changed; therefore, I couldn't get in. I thought about going to my mothers, but I thought that was pushing it. Now here I am at Nelly's sister house and I ain't going nowhere. Her family loves me and like I told her, if she opens her mouth, I'm gonna really kill her.

"Ivan, I know you're jealous of your brother but is all this necessary? Why not leave?" I turned my head.

"Why do you care? Remember, my dick is little and you were only around for the money."

"Ivan, you having a smaller dick then most men don't mean anything. You're not the only one and regardless if I love you or not, you have a good heart; around me anyway until you did this." She pointed to her body.

"Why are you sitting around thinking of ways to get your brother? We both know you won't win going up against him."

"Let me find out you care."

"Of course I care even though I shouldn't after what you did but I guess this is my karma for what happened years ago with your brother."

"If I can get the duffle bag back with the money in it, would you run away with me?"

"No."

"WHAT?" I caught an attitude.

"I wouldn't run away with you because you're a wanted man and I don't wanna be around if they find you. Ivan just leave and never look back." I sat there thinking about the things she said. Could I leave and get over it? *Never mind that.* Did I want to?

"What are you doing?" Nelly asked when I closed the bedroom door and locked it.

"I need some pussy Nelly and…"

"No."

"Come on. Don't be like that." I pulled my dick out and stroked it in front of her.

"If I suck you off will you leave?"

"Maybe but I wanna fuck."

"Ivan, I can't. My body is in a lot of pain and…" I rammed my dick in her mouth to shut her up and enjoyed the feeling she was giving me.

"Yea Nelly. You know how I like it." I ran my hand over her head and pumped in and out but not hard.

"Shit, you're gonna make me cum." Just as I was about to release, she grabbed my balls and held them tight. I was able to pull back before she could go further. It hurt but not like it could've had she squeezed a little tighter. Her body was still weak so her strength wasn't there.

"I want you to leave and never come back or I swear the cops will know you did this."

"Bitch, are you crazy." I punched her and watched her body hit the ground. Who the fuck did she think she was?

"You know I hate doing myself." I stroked my dick over and over until I came and squirted all over her.

"Stop it Ivan." She tried to cover her face but it was too late.

"I'll be back and if you or your family try any shady shit, I will kill you and them." I kneeled down and stared at her.

"Like I said. I wanna fuck so your ass better be ready when I come back. Do I make myself clear?" She cried and nodded at the same time.

"I have someone watching this house and I placed recorders all through here so don't try and be slick." I tossed her head back and walked out. I lied. I ain't have a soul working with me, nor did I place any recorders throughout the house. I don't even have the means to do no high-tech shit like that but she's dumb and will believe it.

"Hey honey. How's she doing?" Her mom asked getting out her car.

"She literally just took some pain pills and fell asleep."

"Oh ok. I'll come back later then." She gave me a hug and got back in her car. I was happy because its no telling if Nelly is still on the floor. I waved, followed out behind her and went to my next destination.

****

"Sir, do you think you'll be needing anything else?" The lady at the hardware store asked. I was picking up rope and duct tape for my mother who I found out through the news, she survived a brutal attack as they say. I have no idea how because I literally beat the crap outta her worse than I did Nelly. She must've been stronger than I thought, or my stupid ass pops came home and found her.

"No this is fine." I only had two hundred dollars on me and didn't wanna spend it all. Remi put a damn hold on my account, which told me my mother opened her fucking mouth. Not only am I gonna kill her the next time, I'm gonna make sure I grab his credit cards first. Don't ask me how but I'm gonna get them. He won't freeze his own assets and by the time he finds out at least, I'll have some money.

"Ok. That'll be $10.53." I handed her a twenty and walked to my car.

"Hey Ivan." I turned and saw Nelly's sister. She was just as pretty and stayed flitting with me any chance she got.

"What up?" I tossed the bag in the back and leaned against my car.

"Nothing. Did you visit my sister?"

"Yea. I'll be back over later."

"Oh yea." She smiled with her index finger hanging out the side of her mouth.

"You need something?" She glanced down at my dick and told me to follow her. I hopped in my car and met her behind some alley. The building was abandoned and there was a vacant lot on the other side. She hopped in my car, asked me to push my seat back, pulled her pants and panties down and literally jumped on my dick.

"Wow. I guess you really wanted this." I said grabbing her waist as she grinded in circles.

"I've wanted you for a long time, but you were stuck under my sister. Shit, Ivan you feel good."

"Is my dick big?" I asked tryna see if Nelly was lying.

"Its good enough for me. Sssss. I'm gonna cum." She continued riding and at some point, she squeezed her pussy muscles and made me cum hard as hell.

"Pretty good ma." We started kissing, moved to the back seat and fucked the shit outta each other. By the time we were finished, both of us were tired. I followed her to her house, took a shower and went to sleep in her bed, with her snuggled up under me. *Nelly who?*

Remi

"Ok mommy. Are you ready to see your baby? Is he daddy? Hi, I'm doctor Gerald and we're going to set Ms. Carter up to see the baby. Are you two excited?" I looked at Naima and her mouth hadn't left the floor. When she woke up, I was the only one here and no one came in. She was as shocked as me learning about being pregnant. He turned some machine on and placed stuff on the ultrasound thing.

"You are seven weeks pregnant mommy and here is the heartbeat." He turned the screen towards us and the volume going louder to hear my child only made this surreal.

"That's my baby?" I pointed to the screen.

"If you're the daddy, then yes." I gave the doctor a look.

"You didn't answer when I asked. You could be the brother, a new boyfriend or..."

"A'ight yo! I get it. But I'm the father."

"Relax Remi. He's only joking." Naima squeezed my hand.

"Loosen up. You both went through some trauma over the last few days. Let this baby be the happiness you're looking for. This attitude isn't good." He pulled the thing out, unplugged the machine and washed his hands.

"Don't you dare say anything." Naima said in a low voice, but I heard her.

"You not the boss of me." I smiled and pecked her on the lips.

"I'm not?"

"Sometimes." I leaned closer to her ear.

"In the bedroom when you bossing me around about how you want it, is the only time." She busted out laughing.

"Thank you." I said to the doctor and shook his hand.

"Keep bossing him around. Maybe it'll loosen him up." He walked out grinning at my girl.

"Are doctors even supposed to say that?"

"Probably not but who cares? Are you happy? You got what you wanted." She pulled the blanket up.

"Hell yea I am." My expression changed.

"I have to find these motherfuckers fast now."

"Remi please be careful, I don't wanna lose you." I could see fear on her face. I sat in bed next to her.

"I'm always careful plus your crazy ass cousins and uncles are already on board." I had a grin on my face.

"What's that grin for?" I went to speak and some chick walked in.

"Who the fuck are you?" She pulled out a gun and pointed it at Naima.

"What the...?" My girl shouted as I hopped over her. My stomach was in pain, but I didn't care.

"You got two seconds to explain who sent you or your brains gonna be on the floor." I knocked the gun outta her hand and had mine on her temple. Hell yea I had Cat bring me one. I didn't know someone would come in here but I'm glad I thought ahead.

"This is the bitch who had my husband killed." She was shaking and crying.

"Your husband?"

"Yes, my husband. Some men broke in my house claiming my father threatened to kill you."

"Julio's your father?" She nodded.

"Sorry to tell you but he's a dead man too." I responded with no remorse.

"Please don't kill me. I have four kids and..." I cocked the gun. I didn't care about her family.

"Remi don't..."

"Naima she tried to kill you. If I wasn't here, she would've and then what?" She moved the covers off her legs and stood.

"I don't think she's gonna do anything stupid knowing either her or her kids can be murdered. Isn't that right?" She shook her head crying.

"Naima."

"Please Remi. She has kids." I blew my breath, snatched her up and made her sit. I sent a message to Ritchie and asked him to come get her.

I knew all about the murder of her husband because it was a plot to get her. Julio needed to suffer since he's trying his hardest to take my girl out. It's unfortunate this woman has kids who are gonna miss their father, but she has no one to blame but her own. He's the reason her husband was taken away and her too if she doesn't comply. Ain't nobody playing games with her or Julio.

****

"You know pregnant women are emotional and Naima wasn't gonna let you kill anyone in front of her." My father said. They placed my mom on a regular floor, and we were waiting for the nurse to finish washing her.

"Man, I wanted to send a message to Julio." I looked at my father.

"Do you know she made me promise I wouldn't kill her before Ritchie came?"

"Did you agree?"

"She said some things in my ear, and I couldn't refuse, so yea." He started laughing as we went in the room to see my mother.

"I never thought I'd see the day a woman had you stuck but I like it. She's giving me a grand baby and hopefully more, along with a wedding." My mom said.

"Can we get the baby out first?" I thought about marrying Naima but with everything going on, it was the last thing I'm thinking of.

"You should run down to city hall and get a quick one so the baby can have your name. I'm just saying." Me and my father shook our heads.

"Ivy pushed the wedding up. It's in a few weeks." I told them. Ivy was scared something would go wrong and didn't wanna waste anymore time marrying Cat. She said it's like they're married anyway so why not get it over with. In five years, she can have a big one.

"A few weeks! What if I'm not out by then?" My mother loved Ivy for Cat like everyone else did.

"The doctor says you can go home at the end of the week. You'll be there and you know Ivy won't have it without you."

"I need a dress and..."

"Naima and Ivy are going out for dresses in a few days. Pops gave them your sizes and before you say it, they're not gonna put you in anything ugly."

"They better not."

"Look. I have to go because Naima is being discharged today. I'll be back up later and pops let me know if you need a break."

"I had a break for over twenty years, I'm good." I kissed my mother's cheek and gave him a pound. I went in the hall, pressed the button to go get Naima and saw this dude who resembled Ivan. I started to chase him but then realized Naima was upstairs.

"SHIT!" I hauled ass up the steps. Fuck an elevator. When I stepped in the room, she had tears in her eyes which meant mine weren't deceiving me.

Naima

"You think getting away will stop me from coming after you and my family?" I froze coming out the bathroom. How did he find me and why is he here?

"Why are you here Ivan?" I felt him behind me and jumped.

"Remi must not love you if you're unprotected."

"I'm not unprotected." I lied and he knew it. Remi went down to visit his mother, so it wasn't a full lie. He was gonna wait but I knew once the doctor said I could go, I'd wanna go home.

"I know you didn't expect the old ass security dude to protect you." He laughed.

"I told him you were my sister and he let me right in. Talking about he's going to the bathroom and grab a coffee. I could kill you ten times by now." Why did he think this was a joke?

"Let my brother know I'm not done, and I'll be back." He kissed the back of my neck and my first reaction was a smack in the face. He grabbed my wrist and threw me against the wall.

"I really thought you learned your lesson." He backhanded me and I felt my nose start to bleed.

"When he's dead, it'll be you and I." He kissed my lips and walked out the room. I rushed in the bathroom and started cleaning my nose and scrubbing my face. I'll be happy when Remi gets him.

I stepped out the bathroom and started putting my clothes on. I'm getting discharged today but there's no more waiting.

"What happened?" Remi rushed in the room, held me in his arms and I started shaking. I explained what went down and the things Ivan told me.

"Get your stuff. We're not staying any longer." I nodded and hurried to gather my things.

"Ms. Carter the doctor hasn't discharged you yet." One of the nurses said.

CLICK! Remi had his gun on the nurse forehead.

"This is the second time y'all whack asses allowed someone in my girl room to attack her." Everyone stopped and stared. Remi cocked the gun.

"I remember you from the last time. Do you remember what I said?" She swallowed hard and let tears fall down her face.

"I said, I'll knock your fucking teeth out if it happened again, didn't I?"

"Sir, I'll discharge her right now." The doctor came behind her.

"Do that and you." He pointed to the nurse.

"You're the manager on this floor, which makes you liable. If I were you, I'd get a lawyer because I'm about to sue the fuck outta this hospital." The doctor gave her a dirty look.

"Sign here Ms. Carter." Naima did like he asked and grabbed my hand.

"Baby lets go."

"You fucked up bitch." He mushed her in the forehead with the gun so hard, she fell back.

"Doc, let the administrators know my lawyers will be contacting them." He nodded.

"Nurse, my office." She looked at him.

"NOW!" Everyone jumped and Remi laughed with his petty ass. I pressed the elevator and we stepped on.

"Expect someone to contact you because they'll wanna settle this. Something of this nature can't get out."

"Whatever you say babe." My arms were around his waist.

"I'm sorry he got to you. Security was supposed to be at your door. Matter of fact, where was he?"

"It doesn't matter. It's over and I'm safe. Let's go home and make up for these last few days."

"You sure?" He asked and I really wasn't, but I needed to distract him.

"Positive." We strolled off the elevator hand in hand. I surveyed the parking lot before walking out. Ivan and Julio are lurking, and I don't wanna be caught out there.

****

"You sure this is what you wanna do?" I asked my mother who decided to meet up with Julio and return the ring. She stopped by the house to see me this morning.

Remi was out with Cat tryna decide who set Ivy up and figure out where Ivan is. He was hiding well, and it only made me more paranoid.

"If its gonna stop him from this bullshit, then of course. I'll never purposely put you in danger."

"What aren't you telling me?" I saw concern on her face. My mother never could hide things from me. She hid the ring situation pretty good, but I never had a reason to question her about it.

"Julio wants you to dead because I should've never had kids with anyone else." Remi told me that but I didn't wanna believe him.

"So, you're telling me even if you give him the ring he's still going to come after me?" I asked not believing a man would be this childish.

"He's very petty." She shook her head.

"Fuck this. I'm going to see Mario. He has to have some information on Julio's whereabouts or something. This man can't be untouchable." I headed towards the stairs.

"Remi know you're going to see him?" I stopped at the steps.

"No and he doesn't care." She gave me a look.

"Remi knows I don't want Mario."

"That's not the point Naima. You're in a relationship with a man who's going outta his way to keep you safe and the first thing you wanna do is see your ex. The ex who wants you back and tried to save you outside the hospital. The ex who will get his ass beat if you allow him to even kiss you on the cheek."

"I just want to ask him and..."

"Its not a good idea honey." She looked at me.

"Do you want Mario or still have feelings for him?"

"Absolutely not!" I answered in a quickness. It's no feelings whatsoever for Mario in my heart. Of course I had love for him but my entire being belonged to Remington Stevens III. I assumed my mom would know that.

"All I'm saying is, let your man handle everything." She had her hands on the side of my face.

"Oh, like he's been doing?" My mother's mouth dropped.

"Since I've been with him, his brother has violently attacked me, kidnapped and threatened to kill me on multiple occasions. Then, I have another person attempting to kill me no thanks to you and your secrets."

"Hold the hell up." My mother put her hand up.

"Hey y'all." I heard Ivy coming through the door. We are supposed to pick up the dresses today.

"Had you not been holding this stupid ring and just gave it up when he asked, I wouldn't be dealing with this."

"NAIMA!" Ivy shouted but I wasn't finished. She had no idea what was going on and it really wasn't her place to say anything.

"The man you used to fuck wants me dead." I walked over to my mother.

WHAP! She smacked the hell out of me.

"I will beat the shit outta your ass Naima Carter if you ever in your got damn life speak to me like that again."

"Did you just smack me?" I asked in disbelief.

"Hell yea and I'm gonna do more than that if you even think to get smart or throw up your hands." Ivy stood in between us.

"Just who in the fuck do you think you are? Huh? I'm not Remi's mother and you're not Ivan. I'll choke the shit outta you before I allow you to disrespect me." She moved closer.

"Ma, I..."

"Save the lame apology for someone else. Let me say this before I walk out." She snatched her things.

"You're in an unfortunate situation due to a man's jealousy on both parts and I'm sure it's affecting you in a bad way, but don't ever assume it's ok to come for me. You know how I get down and

Ivy, Margie, and even Remi won't be able to stop me from beating your ass."

"Nyeemah. Come on now." Ivy tried to calm her down. We both knew how my mother could get.

"Ivy, I love you like I birthed you myself but there's never been a time in my life where I wanted to kill my own child like I do right now. It's best for me to leave." I've never witnessed my mother this upset with me and honestly, it's tearing me up.

"I'll contact Remi when I wanna see my grand baby and I wish the fuck you would fight it." I wiped the tears falling down my face.

"All the things we're doing out here to keep you safe, and it's not enough for you."

"But they still got me and..."

"Why don't you ask yourself how they got you?"

"Nyeemah you got everything." Ivy asked before my mom could say anything. I think she was tryna keep my mom from saying certain things but why? Did she feel the same?

"No Ivy, she needs to hear it. Maybe her ungrateful ass will appreciate the hard work others are doing to avoid it happening again." She opened the front door.

"Mario may have had a reason to treat you the way he did in order to save you."

"What?"

"Even though you didn't know at first, you stayed. Stayed to be disrespected; stayed for him to give you diseases and to get your house taken." I sucked my teeth.

"Ivan started treating you like shit because you were being a bitch over a fucking light that you could've waited for him to change." I couldn't believe she was bringing it up.

"Let's not forget at the grand opening you went to get the liquor and sent security and the worker upstairs, making you vulnerable to a man who attacked you in his brothers other club." I couldn't say anything because she was right. I didn't look at it the way she did, but I understood how it probably looked from other people's point of view.

"I know if it were me, I would've had someone grab Remi right away. Then, you allow some bitch to break y'all up over a video we all knew was a set up; especially when it came from the exact brother who can't stand you."

"What you tryna say?" Now I was aggravated because it seemed like she was accusing me of wanting these bad things to happen.

"Ok y'all. Let's stop this." Ivy continued tryna intervene, but my mom kept going.

"You hear about Remi's mother and instead of going in the hospital like he asked, you decided to park the truck. A truck valet could've parked and what happened? You get abducted by the brother again. One would think y'all were working together since you keep ending up in the same place with him."

"You want me to walk you out Nyeemah?" Ivy asked pushing her to the door.

"One last thing Ivy and I'm going." My mother gave me a sad look but still spoke firmly.

"The shit with Julio is unfortunate because I had no idea he was still searching for the ring and wanted you dead. But your man risked his life running to that van for you. He was devastated

thinking you were in there and what's the first thing you wanna do?"
I put my head down.

"Tell Ivy what you want to do." Ivy turned to me.

"Oh wait! I will. She wants to go see Mario and find out if he knows where Julio is; placing herself in harm's way again."

"Naima."

"It means everyone will have to figure out a way to save you. So my question to you is, are you that selfish you're willing to purposely place yourself in danger in hopes someone will get to you in time? Do you require that much attention?"

"Naima, why are you tryna see him? You know Remi won't be ok with that."

"I'll see you at the wedding Ivy." My mother looked me up and down, rolled her eyes and slammed the door. *Well damn!*

Ivy

I stared at Naima who stood there stuck after her mom cursed her out. Over the years, I've witnessed Nyeemah go off on her quite a bit, but I've never seen her mom this upset. I mean you could hear the anger in her voice and the hurt was written on her face.

I don't know the reason of the argument and it didn't matter because at the end of the day, she is her mom and deserves respect. I could see if she were like these ratchet moms out here who treated her like shit but it's not the case.

"What's going on Naima? Why were you disrespecting your mom?" I wasn't gonna waste time tryna figure it out.

"I don't know what happened." I gave her the side eye.

"I'm serious. I mentioned the ring situation…"

"No, you blamed her for it."

"Well she blamed me for getting in those sticky situations." I limped away because she was being extra. I had a brace on my foot now and still refused to use the crutches. Even with the towels on them, they still hurt my underarms.

"You feel the same?" I turned and saw her arms crossed in front of her.

"Naima if you're looking for me to have your back and say Nyeemah is wrong, I can't." I truthfully told her because everything her mom said, made sense. I'm not saying Nama did it on purpose, but she could've avoided a lot of it.

"Wait a minute. You think I put myself in those situations on purpose?"

"I'm not saying that at all. What I'm saying is, had you handled things differently and not used your *I can fight attitude* it may not have happened."

"What?"

"I don't care about your attitude Naima. Right is right and you had no business speaking to your mother like that." She fell back on the couch.

"I didn't mean to. I'm just tired of being paranoid." I looked at her.

"You think everyone out here ain't tired of the bullshit too? I'm being charged with a crime I didn't even commit. Remi's brother attacked his mother and almost killed her and now this man from your mother's past, wants you dead regardless of the ring. You're not the only one with problems." I rolled my eyes because now she was pissing me off.

"I know Ivy. If I didn't do things my way, I wouldn't be in this." I wasn't comforting her. She knows better.

"Long as you know. Anyway, let's discuss this crap with Ivan attacking his mother. You know Remi's gonna kill him if their father doesn't get him first."

"I know which is another reason I'm nervous. Remi isn't fully healed and..."

"Y'all fucking?" I asked.

"Excuse me!"

"Are y'all fucking?" I asked again.

"Yea but..."

"Then he's fine. A man won't strain himself during sex if he can't take it. The pleasure won't be there because he'll be in too much pain. So again, if y'all fucking then he's fine."

"I guess. Are you ready to get married?" I smiled thinking about the day coming up. I was ecstatic to marry Cat and from what he says, he feels the same.

"Yes, I am lady. Are you ready to have a baby?" I asked because she's been waiting for a very long time. We thought she'd have a baby by Mario after the first year and thank goodness she didn't. Its no telling how much more crap she'd be involved in.

"I am and so is Remi, which is why he's trying his hardest to get Julio and Ivan."

"And the exact reason you need to keep your ass still and apologize to your mother." She waved me off.

"Naima, she's your mother and regardless of how she left out of here, you need to make it right."

"I will after I talk to Remi."

"After you talk to Remi?" I questioned and threw my head back laughing.

"You a fool if you think for one second, he'll be ok or even agree with the way you spoke to Nyeemah."

"I'm not saying he has to agree."

"Then what's the purpose of asking him?" She shrugged her shoulders. I told her to grab her things so we can go. I'm over this childish behavior with her.

****

"What you think?" The guy asked after looking over his tax paperwork. This guy specifically asked for me to look over his finances. I wasn't even supposed to return to work until after my honeymoon.

"You have a lot of expenses to write off but you're still going to owe due to the massive amount of money coming in from this unknown person." I pointed to an account in his bank that showed him receiving large amounts of transfers. He will collect interest on the money but if the individual files their own taxes, he'll be responsible for turning in what its used for. I hated cases like these because they were too messy.

"How about we discuss things over lunch?" He smiled.

"I'm sorry sir. I'm taken." I smiled and showed off my ring. The older gentleman was handsome, and I may have given him a chance if I weren't with Cat. I don't discriminate on age because older men know what they're way around the bedroom.

"Too bad for me but if you ever wanna dip out, my info is in front of you." He stood and gathered his things.

"Oh, let Cat know, he's a lucky man. Him and Remi. Too bad one of you won't make it down the aisle." I moved the chair away from my desk and hurried to the door. I was still in a brace so I couldn't get to him as fast as I wanted.

Unfortunately, no one was in the parking lot at the time. I went to my desk and picked the paperwork up to dial his number. Just my luck the number was a non-working one. Why would he tell me to contact him if I decided to cheat on Cat, knowing the number was incorrect?

I picked my things up from my desk and headed to the door. Something told me to stop and press the alarm on my car. I remembered what happened to Naima and didn't wanna experience the same. When my car didn't blow up, I rushed to get in and sped home. I was so scared, I didn't recognize Cat's car in the driveway. We've been staying at either his moms place or mine because I'm not going home, and the hotel is aggravating sometimes.

"You ok?" He had the door opened before I could place my key in.

"Baby, what does Julio look like?"

"I don't know, why?" I explained what went down at my job and he was livid. He called Remi up quick and twenty minutes later, he was on his way out the door but not without making me go to my mom's. He didn't wanna risk leaving me anywhere alone. The last time someone broke in and they charged me with attacking Remi's mom.

"Be careful babe." I hugged Cat in the room after he placed my suitcase down.

"Your mom better stay at her man's because I'm digging in this later." He squeezed my ass and I wanted him to give me some before he left.

"I think she is."

"Good."

"Don't forget the rehearsal dinner is in a few days and afterwards no sex until the wedding night."

"Bye Ivy."

"What?"

"We're about to get this nigga and you talking about holding out.

I laughed.

"I'm only talking about the night before the wedding."

"Whatever." He slid his tongue in my mouth and his fingers in my pants. I must say, this little release is good enough until he comes home. I locked the door, showered and waited for him to return.

Remi

"Hey babe." I spoke to Naima walking in the bedroom. She was lying down watching TV.

"Hey." I stopped and stripped outta my clothes. It was after nine and I was tired from the running around I had to do. I just wanted to wash, eat dinner and go to bed.

"Babe, I messed up." I heard her saying from the bedroom as I used the bathroom and prepared myself for a shower.

"What you do?" I already knew because Cat told me Ivy mentioned it the other night. I wanted her to tell me, which is why I waited. She doesn't hold secrets as far as I know but what happened between her and her mom took a toll on her. She wasn't really talking, and the sex is just ok, when usually its explosive. I'm not saying she was laying there but its not the same. Its funny how I knew so much about her already.

"I had an argument with my mother and…" She got quiet.

"And what?" I grabbed the soap and started washing myself up. I didn't expect her to get in with me but when she did, I could tell she was crying.

"I was disrespectful and blamed her for the stuff with Julio." I lifted her face.

"Naima, I know it's a pain the ass being paranoid and watching our back but we're doing everything we can to make sure you're safe."

"I know and…"

"Do you because it sounds to me like you're blaming everyone." I started washing her up. Ivy told Cat how she was saying no one was keeping her safe. That shit pissed me off because she had no idea of the things we were doing.

"I just want it all to be over."

"And we don't? You think we want you paranoid? Ivan attacked my mother and I can't find him. You don't think that's bothering me? Or the fact your mom's ex wants to kill you because you're not his? I mean why are you taking your frustrations out on the people tryna keep you safe?" I rinsed the soap off, stepped out and left her in there. She was starting to aggravate me. I'm all about spoiling my woman but this baby shit ain't what I'm into.

"Remi, she got mad because I wanted to see Mario and find out if he had Julio's number." I swung my body around and gave her the dirtiest look. She tightened the towel around her body and stood there.

"Why the fuck would you even consider doing some shit like that?" Ivy didn't tell Cat about this. If she did and he told me, I damn sure wouldn't have held it in.

"If they're contacting him then…"

"Then its none of your business Naima."

"Excuse me. If Julio's contacting him, how is it none of my business?" I put my boxers on and then my sweats because I'm not sure after this conversation I'd be staying here.

"So what he's contacting your ex over you, who cares? We know why he wants you and so do you. What the fuck will you meeting up with Mario do? It's not gonna stop him from coming after you so tell me, why you feel the need to see him?" She sat on the bed and put her head down.

"You want that nigga Naima?" Her head lifted.

"Tell me right now because I'm not about to be with a woman who finds dumb reasons to see her ex."

"I didn't see him Remi."

"Listen. If you wanna go back to him then so be it. I'm not about to have a conversation over a nigga who did you wrong for whatever reason and wants you back. If that's where you wanna be then go for it. We can co-parent the baby if that's the case." I'm in love with Naima and I'd be hurt if she left but I'm not competing with no man. I've never had to and I'm not about to.

"Remi?" I threw my t-shirt on and made my way down the steps.

"You can stay here for as long as you like. I'm out." I grabbed my keys and opened the door.

"REMI!" She shouted. I closed the door and turned to see what she wanted.

"I'm good Naima." She strolled over to me in just the towel she kept on from the shower.

"I don't wanna fight with you and I'm sorry for suggesting I should see my ex. In no way do I want him." She moved closer and now we were basically touching.

"You are the man I'm in love with and having a baby with. I was trying to help that's all. I'm sorry."

"A'ight." I still needed to go.

"We are never breaking up so you can be mad all you want but its me and you forever." I smirked. I told her that when we first confessed our feelings and I still felt the same, but I meant what I said about not competing with no man.

"You wanna leave and have a drink, fine, but I expect you to make love to me when you return." She turned to walk away and dropped the towel.

"What I tell you about playing?" She looked over her shoulder.

"I'm not playing. You wanna go out and I'm the only woman who'll be in the bed when you return. Me dropping the towel is to remind you of what's waiting." She put her foot on the step and stopped.

"You need something?" She bit down on her lip.

"If you weren't pregnant right now, I'd squirt in you on purpose." I told her, locked he door and carried her up the stairs. I wasn't going nowhere tonight.

****

"If her father was alive, he'd probably beat her ass for talking to Nyeemah like that." My father said and sat down next to my mom.

I was at their house telling them what happened between my girl and her mom. I've been here everyday since my mother came home. The new security system was installed but my mother was still our main priority, so we made sure to have someone around at all times.

Ivan was bold as shit to come here, and I could see him possibly trying again. I asked my mother why she didn't move and her exact words were, *my son is not running me out my own house.*

"She was in her feelings and I get it but you know I had to let her know. Not only does she owe her mother an apology, she needs to respect our hustle. Shit, we all searching for these bastards."

"She's probably scared. Ivan keeps getting to her and Julio acting like a got damn baby." My father barked as he said the last words. He wanted van and Julio asap.

"I get it but…"

"But what? She's scared y'all. I don't think she should've spoken to her mother like that, but she doesn't know what to do." My mom chimed in.

"I have to agree with Nyeemah tho son and I don't care if you get mad." My father said.

"About?"

"Some of the shit with Ivan could've been avoided. I'm not saying he should've taken things as far as he did, but Naima played a part in his reactions." I nodded.

Naima does have a mouth on her and probably didn't expect my brother to come for her. She knows now, just like Nelly learned. I'm not saying he was right, and he will deal with the consequences, but I do wish my girl held her tongue at times. She's not ratchet but even I have to let her know it's too much at times.

"What you wanna do now?"

"I don't know. All we can do is wait Ivan out because he's coming back at some point." I said with conviction. He's broke and will need money.

"You think so?"

"Yup. He may not come here but he will return." I kissed my mother on the cheek and gave me father a pound. I had to meet Cat to get some other shit done.

"Aren't y'all too old for hickeys?" My mom blushed.

"You haven't seen the rest of her body. Boy, she has them…"

"Remington stop. You know he hates when you speak like that." My face was turned up.

"Ma, you supposed to be hurt."

"I am and so are you. Have you and Naima had sex?" She asked with a straight face.

"Exactly! Bye son. I love you." She blew me a kiss and I walked out laughing. I'm happy as hell my pops is home. They missed each other and its about time they enjoyed each other's company again.

Cat

"Where is Ivan?" Remi has his gun pressed against Monee's forehead. Ritchie wanted to kill her the first day they picked her up, but Remi asked him not to. He wanted to question her himself.

"I don't know. I swear I don't." She cried.

"Let me show you what he did to my mother." Remi pulled his phone out and showed her a picture. Monee gasped and put her head down.

"Now, if you're tryna stay alive I suggest you start talking."

"I don't know where he is."

BAM! Remi split her eye open with his fist and knocked her out.

"Can somebody grab me water to toss on this bitch?" You heard someone turn the faucet on. He threw it on her and she woke up tryna get out the seat.

"Let's try this again. Where's my brother?"

"I swear Remi, I don't know. The day Ritchie picked me up, Ivan left a few minutes before him to grab stuff for your girlfriend."

"What?" He asked her.

"He wanted to clean her up after..." Monee stopped speaking.

"After what?" We all waited to hear what she had to say.

"After I kept hitting her and made her nose bleed."

"You were beating on my girl too?" Remi snatched her out the chair, threw her against the wall and I had to pull him off because he was about to beat her to death."

"I'm sorry Remi. He had this planned for months." She barely got out.

"Say what?"

"When you beat him up for walking in your house, he called me to the hospital and thought of different plans to get you. Then, he tried the restaurant thing with her in the basement." She turned her head and stared at me.

"What?"

"He paid my brother to rob your house and called the cops to say Ivy did that to his mom." She was telling everything thinking Remi would let her live.

"Hold up." I was fuming.

"It was your brother who came to my house. And how did my girl get charged?" Monee was barely breathing at this point.

"He told the cops he saw Ivy running out his mother's house after he did it." I ended up punching her in the face myself.

"That's for Ivy because if she were here, she'd do it." I barked at her.

"Where is he?" Remi was shaking the hell outta her to make her speak.

"I don't know but he's not gonna stop until he destroys you Remi. He's going to burn your businesses and..."

"Did he rape Naima?" She shook her head no. I don't think his girl told him, but he wanted to make sure in case she was embarrassed and scared to mention it.

"He refused to do it and I asked him to. I hate her." That was is it. Remi beat her so bad she was unrecognizable and most likely dead. Her body laid on the ground as we went to wash our hands.

"You a'ight?" Remi asked picking up the paper towels to dry his hands

"Yea but how am I gonna tell the lawyer Monee confessed to Ivan being the one lying about Ivy doing that to your mom?"

"You know she's not going to jail and my mom is awake and talking. Therefore; they can ask her who did it. Ivy's good bro. You know we never thought to question you about her." I nodded.

"And my mom wouldn't be coming to y'all wedding either had she done it."

"Yea. The shit bothers me tho. Like how you attack your mother and blame someone else?" Remi smirked.

"The nigga knew I'd go after whoever did it. If he blamed Ivy, it would take the heat off him. In the eyes of the law, it was an easy escape, but he also didn't expect my mother to get up."

"True. Did big Remi ever get the video?" He ran his hand over his head

"Yea but he won't let me watch it." I gave him the side eye.

"He said it's too bad and had to turn it off himself."

"Damn."

"I know. I can't wait to find his dumb ass." He wanted to murder Ivan and I don't blame him.

"Where you think he could be?" I asked because as of right now we or should I say, I had no idea where.

"He's around here somewhere." I turned to him.

"Not sure where yet but there's been no sign of him at the airports or train station. Plus, I froze his accounts, so he has no money besides this." He lifted a black duffle bag.

"When they found Naima, this was hidden in the closet. I'm sure he went back to the apartment but there's no money. He stuck, which means he'll contact my mother again after he finds out she made it and request money."

"You think so?"

"I'm positive. He's too stupid to know not to." He shrugged and opened the door for us to leave.

"Let's get these suits before your future wife blames me for you not having it." I started laughing

"Yo, thanks for taking care of my cousin." Ritchie shouted to Remi.

We knew Naima's family but not where we'd hang out with them. However; we probably will now because they've been helping a lot. Thank goodness because Remi was still recovering, and I was focused on making sure Ivy didn't stay in jail. It's been a hectic ass year.

"Always. Trust she's in good hands." They gave each other a head nod and we left.

****

"Ok son. You look very handsome." My mom fixed the bow tie on my suit. Today is my wedding day and we had so much security you'd think the president was coming; Obama anyway. He's still my president.

"Thanks." I looked over at my pops who was in a deep conversation with Remi's dad.

"You ok bro?" Remi patted my shoulder.

"I'm good. Just nervous about the Julio shit."

The day Ivy mentioned him stopping by her job, me, Remi and a bunch of other guys went out searching for him. Remi's father even came because he's the only one who really knew what he looked like. Ivy described him but unless I saw him myself, I couldn't tell you anything.

"If he even thinks about circling the block someone will get him. Focus on meeting your wife at the altar." I stood there happy and nervous at the same time. Happy Ivy's about to be my wife but my nerves were shot thinking about Julio and Ivan. I didn't trust either one.

"Time to take your place." The reverend spoke and closed the door.

"I'm proud of you son." My pops said.

"She looks so pretty Joseph." My mother walked in to tell me. It looks like she was crying already.

"At least I know she showed up." She smacked my arm.

"Let's go." I told everyone and spoke to the guests on the way down the aisle.

"Damn yo. No more extra pussy for you." Remi said as the bridesmaids came down the aisle.

"After she left me the last time, I'm good. That shit hurt and I'm not going through it again."

"How we both cursing in this damn church?" We started laughing and both of our mothers gave us a dirty look.

"Please stand." I heard the pastor say and my heart sped up. This was it. The moment I've been waiting for.

"In one million years, I never thought I'd meet someone that's perfect, I never thought that someone could make my mind go around in circles."

The song *Can't Let Go* by Calvin Richardson played, and the doors opened. I couldn't see her at first, but the gasps let me know she wasn't anything short of beautiful. Once Ivy came into view, I now felt the same as the guests. She was breathtaking and just think; my ex almost buried her alive. The closer she got, I could see the tears running down her face.

"You're beautiful." I wiped her eyes and placed a gentle kiss on her lips when she stopped in front of me.

"Are you sure you're ready?" I smiled.

"Never been more ready for anything in my life. I love you Ivy Blackmon." She kissed me and this time Remi had to pull us apart.

"Do that freaky shit in the limo."

"Boy don't be cursing." Ivy shot him a nasty look after saying it.

"Can we get started?" The pastor asked and everyone laughed.

"Absolutely." Me and Ivy turned and let him do the ceremony. I must say the things she said in her vows had me shed a few tears and vice versa.

"Are you happy?" I asked Ivy on the way out the church. We just finished saying thank you to everyone and on our way to the reception.

"Very. Now let's consummate this marriage with a quickie in the limo." I laughed. Even with the small brace on her foot she was still beautiful. We handled our business on the way to the reception. It was a good day so far.

Naima

"After dinner I want you to apologize to your mother." Remi whispered in my ear as we waited for the DJ to introduce the bridal party.

"Remi do we have to do it here?" I whined and poked my lips out.

"Yea because it's been too many days that y'all haven't spoken."

"But..."

"But nothing. Plus, you give me better sex when you're in a good mood." I couldn't believe he said that.

"Huh?"

"When you're aggravated, you do the bare minimum but when you're in a good mood, you go all out." I covered my mouth laughing. He wasn't lying. I loved having sex with Remi but with everything going on, I did the minimum and made him cum fast just so we could be done. It wasn't right but at least there was no need to stray.

"I'm serious." He shrugged.

"Remi and Naima." The DJ shouted for us to step in the dining area. I took my seat next to Ivy and he sat next to where Cat would.

I glanced around and noticed everyone here appearing to be happy. I thought about my wedding and if I'd ever have one. We're about to have a baby but he hasn't asked for my hand in marriage. Not that I'm in a rush but we all know women think too much at weddings. The thought of how your own ceremony will be and what you'd do different is in our heads.

The DJ introduced Ivy and Cat, and everyone clapped. They were the perfect couple and deserved every bit of happiness they are about to receive. The smile on my best friends face only proved that true love exists. I was indeed happy for them.

Once they sat, appetizers were served along with a salad and shortly after; dinner. Remi stood first clinking his glass and did his best man speech. It was touching and I shed a tear listening to him mention Cat being the brother he never had, and the one he considered his own. Those two been through a lot growing up and their bond is solid. Remi told me a while ago, he'd do anything for Cat and that's who his real brother is; not Ivan.

I stood to do my toast and of course me and Ivy cried. She has been my ride or die, along with my mother and now she's married and pregnant. I have no doubt in my mind she'll be the same with her children.

I turned to my mom and smiled as the guy she's been dating whispered something in her ear making her blush. I'm happy she had someone too.

Remi looked at me and gestured with his head for me to go speak. I stuck my tongue out and walked over to her table. She immediately sucked her teeth and rolled her eyes. My mother is a trip.

"Can I speak to my mom alone?" He gave me a hug and stepped off. I took a seat next to her.

"Who told your ass to sit?" She lifted her drink and sipped it.

"Shouldn't you be out looking for your ex or placing yourself in a situation to be saved?" I shook my head because she was being petty.

"I'm sorry for disrespecting you." I rested my head on her shoulder.

"Mmmm hmmm." Her mouth was turned up.

"I should've never spoke to you like that. I was in my feelings because of being paranoid and took it out on you."

"If your father was here, he would've knocked your teeth out." She shook her head in disappointment.

"But he's not." She put her drink down and stared at me.

"You're upset he's not around?"

"Why couldn't anyone save him?" I busted out crying and felt some arms around me.

"Let me take her outside." Remi carried me out the dining area and sat me down on one of the benches close to the door. He said I needed a minute.

"Naima you're pregnant and need to calm down." He whispered in my ear.

"I miss him. I'm never gonna have him walk me down the aisle or..."

"Why is it bothering you so much now? I'm not being mean Naima, but he's been gone for a long time." Remi spoke in his caring voice.

"I've always wanted him around. I guess after finding out the truth when it comes to his death, it's bothering me."

"We did everything we could to save him Naima, but the stab wounds were too deep and we couldn't stop the bleeding." Big Remi stood there with his wife who could barely stand herself. Remi offered her a seat.

"I was there honey and all your father kept saying is for big Remi to watch over you. Keep you and your mom safe. Naima." She had me face her.

"He loved you and your mom dearly and sadly he wasn't able to watch you grow. But you have your mother, Ivy, Margie, your crazy family and now us." I nodded and wiped my face.

"One thing I can say about your father is he would've never allowed you to disrespect your mother." Big Remi said and I stared at my mom.

"Don't look at me. I didn't tell them. I would've waited for you to deliver then whooped your ass." My mother had her hands up. I don't know why it made me upset to find out they knew but it did.

"Regardless of how we found out, it's never ok to speak to the woman who birthed and raised you on her own after the untimely death of your father. Then, you took your time apologizing." Remi's mom made me feel worse than I already did.

"I'm sorry ma and I'll never disrespect you again." I got up to hug her and she fell into me.

"What the hell?" She felt her side and blood was coming out.

"REMI SHE'S BLEEDING!" I screamed but him and his father were gone. His mom walked away as fast as she could and not even a minute later all the guys from inside ran out the door.

"What happened?" Ivy rushed over and so did some woman who claimed to be a physician. She lifted the top to my mother's outfit, and you could see the blood pouring out. The woman took her suit jacket off and started to put pressure on the wound.

"Naima, the ring…" My mom was taking short breaths.

"I don't care about a ring. Stop talking ma and wait for the ambulance." Outta nowhere the glass shattered from the windows and doors and bullets could be heard outside.

"Shit. I have to get my mother outta here." Ivy nodded and grabbed two of the waiters off the ground.

"Please help me take her to the car." Both of them looked scared and wouldn't move.

"You can leave with us." They nodded and lifted my mom. The physician followed behind still applying pressure to my mom's side.

"Shit, where are the keys?" Ivy shouted and ran back in.

"No one's in there. Hop in the limo." Ivy's mom shouted and all of us ran to it. Thankfully, it was in the back with the driver in it. His eyes grew big; yet, it didn't stop him from taking off. He went through red lights the entire way. He parked in front of the ER and I jumped out.

"EXCUSE ME!" All the nurses stared at me when I went inside yelling.

"Are you ok?" Some doctor walking up asked.

"NO! MY MOTHER WAS SHOT AT A WEDDING RECEPTION AND WE NEED HELP GETTING HER IN." The doctor yelled for a tech to grab a stretcher and ran behind me.

"Where was she hit?" The doctor asked and the physician answered as they laid her on the bed.

"In the side and I couldn't find the bullet. Her heartrate is dropping and…" Is all I heard because in my head, my mother was already dead, and I couldn't take it. Ivy asked someone to find me a seat and I'm glad she did because I probably would've passed out.

"You ok?" I stared at Ivy who had a cup of water in her hand and blood on her wedding dress.

"I'm ok. What if she…?" Ivy shushed me.

"She's gonna be fine sis. You know your mom isn't gonna let you be here without both parents." I nodded and my mom's boyfriend walked over to me. I heard him yelling for her back at the reception, but I couldn't stop to tell him where we were. Someone at the place must've mentioned it.

"Is she ok?" He asked kneeling down in front of me.

"We don't know yet." He went to the nurse's desk and spoke to them for a minute. I could hear him asking if they could please have the doctor come out as soon as they know something.

"She's gonna be fine Naima." Ivy hugged me and I prayed she was right. I don't know what I'd do if she died too.

Remi

"Fuck!" I ran out the hall after seeing Nyeemah fall into my girl. I didn't even have time to see if she was ok because I knew Julio had to be the one who did it. Who else would show up here and start shooting? I'm sure he meant to hit my girl because he didn't have the ring yet. In order to retrieve it, her mom had to give it to him.

We had security all through the wedding and reception. I guess he figured since he couldn't get in, he'd shoot through the glass.

"GET DOWN!" My pops yelled out and all of a sudden, we were in a full-fledged attack. This nigga had mad people with him, and the bullets wouldn't stop coming

"Shit, we don't have enough people." I looked and no one was out here besides me and my pops. I never got the chance to run in and get the team.

"We good." Cat came out along with others and shortly after, there were dead bodies on the ground and the black trucks were pulling off.

I ran back in behind Cat searching for Naima. She wasn't there but the blood trickled into the dining area and out the back door. When we made it to where the blood stopped, the limo was gone and so were our women.

"They went to the hospital." Some guy walked out the kitchen with a cart to clean up.

"A'ight. Thanks." Cat asked some of the women who were left to put the gifts in their cars, and he'll pick them up later. He grabbed the money envelopes and I don't blame him. Cat and Ivy were well off, but the money was a gift and theirs, not anyone else's.

I ran to my truck, hopped in and unlocked the door for Cat and my pops. Once we were all inside, I floored it to the hospital. I don't know how the cops missed me and I really don't care because I wouldn't have stopped until we reached my girl anyway.

"I hope she's ok." My father said when we pulled up at the hospital.

"Me too." I responded and ran inside. Naima and Ivy had blood on their dresses and were crying. Ivy's mom was sitting with her boyfriend and Nyeemah's mom new friend. He looked nervous and scared. I would too if someone shot my woman at a wedding.

"How is she?" I asked and Naima ran over to me.

"Someone shot her in the side." I shook my head.

"Who would do this? I mean my mom is rude as hell but never bad where someone should've shot her." Naima cried.

"Julio." We turned around and Mario was coming towards us with a kid.

"Naima." The little girl ran over. Naima didn't hug her due to the blood on her dress but said she'd do it another time.

"Hey sweetie."

"I miss you Naima. When are you and daddy getting married?" I tensed up a little but couldn't get mad. She's a child and her father and Naima were a couple for some years.

"I miss you too and he is my man now." Naima pointed to me and she looked up.

"Oh." She put her head down.

"I'm sure daddy will find a new lady that you'll love." The little girl said ok but continued asking questions.

"Can I talk to you?" Mario asked me and the little girl stayed with Naima.

"Sorry about that." He said and walked out the door.

"She's a kid." I told him

"My kids love Naima and I hadn't mentioned us breaking up. I didn't even think they'd paid attention and assumed they knew because she hasn't been around." He stopped and looked at me.

"First, I wanna say, no disrespect but I appreciate the way you're protecting Naima. It's better than I've ever been able to." You could tell in his voice he missed her but too bad. She's mine.

"Also, I can tell she's very happy with you."

"She better be." I joked.

"Nah, she is. The way she looks at you is of pure love." He stared through the window at her.

"A'ight yo. I know my girl used to be with you but I'm not tryna get into conversations about the past. Why you want me to follow you out here?"

"Julio has been watching Naima."

"How the fuck you know?"

"Because he called me this morning to say he's going to get her at the wedding." I yoked him up and saw Cat and my pops running out the hospital.

"Why didn't you call?"

"Bro, she changed her number. I lost my phone when some dude stabbed me in the side for tryna save her and I didn't know where the wedding was."

"Oh." I let him go.

"Look, I don't want anything bad to happen to Naima either but Julio's not gonna stop until he gets whatever he's searching for." I ran my hand down my face.

"He wants the ring and to kill her."

"I thought he only wanted the ring." He asked in a confused tone.

"Evidently, Naima's mom shouldn't have had any kids if they weren't by him." He gave me the side eye.

"Exactly. He got her mom tonight which I'm sure is an accident."

"Damn. I have a number for you." He pulled his phone out. Now it was my turn to give him the side eye.

"I have no clue how he got my new number but when he called earlier, he must've forgot to block his number." He read the number off and I made sure to lock it in my phone.

"Remi, I don't want any hard feelings towards us. The best man won, and I won't disrespect the relationship you and Naima have." I stared and asked him why he said it.

"Once y'all get Julio this will be over; we may see one another in passing and my kids may be with me. We don't have to speak but I also don't wanna watch my back when you walk past."

"I'm not a weak nigga Mario and if I want someone, I'll get him. I don't do the talking shit and trust if I really wanted to get at you, I would've done it." He nodded.

"As far as the kids, I'd never approach a man around them. They're innocent in this fucked up game. Plus, when Naima delivers I don't wanna think about anyone harming her or my kids."

"Congratulations. I didn't know."

"We recently found out and thanks." I went to walk away and turned around.

"Oh. No need to contact her; not that you can with her changing her number but still. She has a man and anything you need to say to her, can be said to me."

"I respect it." I stepped in the hospital as the doctor came out. He grabbed his daughters' hand and walked out. I asked Naima why was he there and she said, his father is still there and they were visiting. I had to make sure he wasn't following her.

"Ms. Carter is going to be fine." The doctor spoke.

"Surgery is done?" Naima asked.

"No. She's still under but the surgeon wanted me to inform the family, she was hit on the side by a bullet, but it came out somehow. In any case, no major arteries were hit and once they're finished, she'll be out." Nyeemah's boyfriend shook the doctor's hand and I hugged my girl.

"She's ok ma. Let me get you home to change."

"But..."

"Naima your dress is full of blood and you need to relax before seeing her."

"I'm not leaving Naima. I'll call if anything changes." Her mom's boyfriend said and I carried her to my truck.

"You seem to be in a better mood." I said and smirked.

"Whatever. I'll give you some now that I know she'll be fine." Her head was on the seat.

"Nah. I don't want it." She turned to me.

"I don't like the way you said it, so it won't be good. You'll be doing it just to satisfy me." She tried to undo my jeans and I popped her hand.

"Don't touch me with blood on you." She started laughing.

"Let me find out my man has a petty side to him too."

"Yup. Now when we get home, take a shower and I'll be waiting for you naked."

"I thought you said, you didn't want it." She was smirking.

"I changed my mind." She laughed so hard, she had to grab her stomach. We drove to the house and I carried her in and straight to the bathroom. I ended up getting in the shower with her and lets just say, she was in a very good mood.

****

"You ready to do this?" I asked my father who was with us.

The day Mario gave me the number Julio contacted him from, I had a trace put on it and sure enough, it led us straight to him. I didn't know at first until my father decided to ride along and see if it was the same man. Once he told me yes, we started putting things in place to get him.

At first, I assumed he'd stay with his daughter and her kids since we took away her husband. Fortunately for him, he stayed elsewhere which kept his daughter safe for the moment. I give it to her though; she refused to offer up any information regarding him. It's sad because now the four kids have no parents. I promised Naima I wouldn't kill her, but Cat didn't. Her death wasn't too bad but then again, a bullet to the head usually kills a person on impact and it did. No suffering for her; yet, the kids will in the long run.

"Let's get this bastard." My father said in the car and we all made sure to check our weapons. We were gonna get Julio sooner but like I said, we wanted to plan everything out perfect, get a positive ID and wait on Cat. He was adamant about us not going in without him and asked us to wait until he returned from his honeymoon. That's why I loved him more than my own blood brother. He had my back at all times and vice versa.

"A'ight." I stepped out the car to make sure everyone was in position. The place Julio was held up in is huge and I didn't want any mistakes or to lose anyone. We've been a team for a very long time and I knew their families. I didn't wanna be the one to relay one of their sons died fighting to keep my woman and her mom safe.

"The house has five bedrooms, a huge backyard and various entries. Make sure to cover them all and inside, be careful because he had security in there as well." The guys nodded.

"Make sure your vests are tight and do not leave anyone behind." They all nodded again, and I wished them good luck. This is a mission we haven't done in a very long time because of being out the game. Make no mistake; we're still thorough as hell.

"They good?" My father asked and I told him and Cat yes.

We drove two streets over from where Julio was at, shut off the lights and got out. Each of us were dressed in black and being it was almost midnight, no one could see anything. On the walk over, I noticed Cat texting.

"Tell Ivy you're fine." He started laughing.

"Shit, your girl is over there worrying her to death about you." I started laughing.

"It's because I haven't responded to her text. Ivy knew her husband would answer." I joked and my father shook his head laughing.

"Damn right punk. My wife won't hold out on me because of yo ass." I waved him off. When we made it to the street, everyone became silent.

"It's finally time to get this punk." My father whispered and we all looked.

"He should've been dead years ago." He cocked back his gun and stormed straight to the front.

"Here we go." All the lights were out except the kitchen one. I used my elbow to break the side window by the front door. I expected to hear an alarm or something but nope. Either they didn't have one or someone forgot to turn it on.

I reached in, unlocked the door and we stood at the doorway. It was weird no one was around. I used my index finger to gesture for them to follow me.

Once we stepped in the living room area, at least six security dudes were on the couch and floor knocked the hell out. What kinda people he had working for him? All of us put a bullet in them. My father made his way up the stairs and to the room we were told they'd be in.

Sylvia, who is Julio's daughters' mother is the one who answered the cell phone when I called. Who knew she was already plotting on him after finding out he's the one who possibly had her daughter murdered? We met up with her, set this up and here we are. In the house of the man who tried to murder my girl and shot her mother.

"I got this." My father said and walked in the room alone. We weren't worried about anything happening because security was dead and if Sylvia acted stupid then he'd end her too.

Julio

"What the fuck?" I barked at the stupid motherfuckers working with me. I was still pissed about the situation at the wedding. It's been a couple of weeks and I heard Nyeemah finally got out the hospital.

"Y'all were supposed to shoot the daughter."

"Boss, we thought it was her." I tossed back the drink in my hand.

"Fuck!" I slammed the glass down on the table making it shatter and left them standing there. All I could think about is how Nyeemah and I were the last time we saw one another.

"Nyeemah, I don't know how it happened." I stood against the window staring as she cried her eyes out after hearing about the other chick I impregnated. The bitch saw us together and blurted it out all because I wouldn't fuck her any longer.

"You know how it happened Julio. You fucked her and now she's having your child. How could you do that to me?" I moved closer and lifted her face. Her eyes were blood shot red, snot trailed down to her top lip and her body shook from crying so hard.

"I'm sorry Ny." That's the nickname I gave her.

"I had a weak moment and..."

WHAP! She smacked me hard and I grabbed her wrists.

"I said I was sorry."

"Sorry isn't going to make this child go away. In three months, she'll give birth to your first born." I let go of her wrists and plopped down on the loveseat across from her.

"How long did you know?" I didn't answer.

"How long?" I blew my breath.

"When she turned two months." I felt a pillow hit my head.

"You knew this entire time and didn't tell me?"

"I didn't know how Ny."

"You know why Julio." She wiped her face.

"You knew I'd leave you for it." I watched her stand and run upstairs. I followed and prayed she wasn't doing anything stupid.

"What are you doing?" I kept taking out the clothes she put in the suitcase.

"I can't be with a man who's expecting a child with the woman he cheated on me with. I won't do it."

"Ny, don't do this." I stopped her from packing and forced her to look at me. It was killing me to see how much pain she was in.

"Julio, Stop." She all but moaned out when I kissed her neck.

"You're not leaving me." I stripped her down, laid her on the bed and made love to her. When we finished and she fell asleep, I woke her up and made love to her again. I needed her to know I was in love with her and refused to lose her.

"I love you Julio." I heard and felt a kiss on my cheek. Being half sleep, I thought it was a dream until I woke up the next day and she was nowhere to be found.

I searched daily for her and nothing. I threatened anyone who knew her, and they all swore not to have seen her. Unfortunately, I was locked up shortly after, so my search ended.

It wasn't until years later when I was released from prison did I hear about her new relationship to some guy. Supposedly, they were madly in love and had a child. I was furious because she and I should've conceived with one another.

Anyway, we were out one day, and my brother was going on and on about how he lost the ring my father gave him gambling. My mother cursed him out because she said he had no business even bringing the ring. He vowed to get it back and low and behold we ran into the guy he lost it to. How ironic it was the same dude my ex Ny had a child with? We ended up fighting and he lost his life in the process. We still don't have the ring, I don't have Ny and her bastard child is still alive.

In the beginning, I wanted her dead because she wasn't mine but changed my mind. Her daughter had nothing to do with our past. That's until my daughter and her husband were murdered. I knew it was Remington or his son because of the explosion outside the hospital. I figured they'd get me back, but I had no idea they knew about my daughter.

I made it my business to set Naima's murder up at the wedding. I knew she'd be there because Ivy is her best friend, who by the way was gorgeous and had she played into my hand at her office, I definitely would've fucked her.

Now I'm sitting in my ex Silvia's house; my daughters mother watching her give me head and thinking about Nyeemah being the one to do it. I've never gotten over her and after this is over with, I'm still gonna shoot my shot with her. Fuck the dude she's with now. He's not me and I know she missed me, the same way I missed her.

"Mmmm. Shit woman." I pumped harder in her mouth and came so hard, I fell back on the bed. After a few minutes, she got me hard again and the two of us fucked like old times.

****

"What the fuck is going on?" I felt something cold on the front of my forehead and stared into the eyes of Remington Stevens. How the fuck did he get in here; especially with the amount of security I had?

"You got our daughter murdered." I slid my eyes to the right and this bitch had her back against the headboard smoking a cigarette.

"What?"

"Before she was taken from me, she called and said you had her husband murdered. At first, I didn't believe her until that ex bitch name came up." She hates Nyeemah because even though I cheated, I never left her and didn't plan on it. Hell, if Ny agreed to be my daughters' mother, I would've killed Sylvia a long time ago

"She said you were after her daughter and some ring."

"Sylvia hold on." I tried to get up but Remington busted my nose with the gun.

"You couldn't leave her alone. Now I have to raise my four grand babies because of your stupidity. Why couldn't you leave the past in the past?" She hopped out the bed and my body was drug off by my feet, down the steps and out the door.

"Hello Julio." I heard and turned around to see Nyeemah standing there looking beautiful as ever.

"Hold on. You didn't say anything about bringing this bitch to my house." Sylvia shouted, letting me know she's been working with them.

"Sylvia you slept with a man who had a woman, kept the baby to spite me and after all these years, one would think you'd be happy because you had the man. Yet, you're bitching because I'm outside your house?" Sylvia couldn't say shit. Nyeemah was right. All these years and she still salty.

"You got one more time to call me out my name and my son in law will put one in your head." She pointed to Remi's son who had a grin on his face. I had no idea their kids were engaged.

"Julio, I thought you were over me when I left you."
Nyeemah walked up on me as I laid on the ground in a pair of boxers.

"Nyeemah, I never got over you."

"I'm sorry to hear that. You tried to kill my daughter for not being yours and brought all this drama to our front door and for what? Because you wanted me back?" She asked.

"I'll do it all over again if I thought you'd come back to me."

"You should've stayed away." She nodded her head at Remington, and he started raining blows on me. When I thought he was finished, more came.

"You're gonna die the same way my best friend did." Remington said in my ear.

"AHHHHH!" I shouted as he repeatedly stabbed me. All I could do is lay there until blackness took over.

Ivan

"Keep going sexy. I'm about to cum." I pumped harder in Nelly's sisters' mouth and released all I had. She was even sexy swallowing.

"Joy, can I borrow your…" Nelly stopped short after opening the door and catching us naked. I've been staying here everyday and not once did Nelly catch us. After she got better, she went back to work and the two of us would have sex here and there. I never mentioned sleeping with her sister and had she not caught us, I still wouldn't have.

"Really Joy? Ivan, I can't believe you would do me like this after everything we been through." I zipped my jeans up.

"Why not? You fucked me and my brother. It's only fair to return the favor." She shook her head and stepped out the room.

"Fuck her Ivan." She got in the bed and pulled the covers up.

"I'll be back." She waved me off. I walked in Nelly's room and found her crying. Was she upset over me sleeping with her sister?

"Why you upset?" She turned over.

"Because I don't wanna be in this situation with you and you're forcing me too. Then, I find out you're fucking my sister."

"Nelly, why does it matter? You don't love me and if I'm fucking her, then I won't bother you." In my head it made sense.

"You don't have to deal with me and at least I'm not bringing another woman here."

"Ivan, just go."

"Nah. I don't want you upset." I sat next to her.

"Look, your sister has been coming onto me for years. I never took the bait until recently. If you want the truth, your pussy feels way better than hers and you definitely suck dick better." I was lying. They both had some banging ass pussy and they were in a tie on who sucked me off the best.

"Ivan." I lifted her up and wrapped her legs around my waist.

"Its been about you all these years Nelly and ain't shit gonna change." She put her tongue in my mouth. For someone who seemed upset a few minutes ago, she damn sure got down, locked the bedroom door and stripped.

"I'm not sucking your dick and use this baby wipe to clean it off." She passed me those Scott wipes you see on the back of toilets. I wiped my dick off like she asked.

"Fuck me good Ivan." She laid back on the bed with her legs open and I gave her what she wanted. She did moan louder than normal. I had no doubt it was to let her sister know she was fucking me. It didn't matter to me and I'm sure it don't matter to Joy because she knows we still gonna do us.

"You feel better?" I asked Nelly as we stepped out the shower together.

"Yea. I'm getting my own place." I looked at her.

"I found an apartment across town and they're letting me move in this weekend. You coming?"

"If you want me too."

"Ivan, we were good together until you had a hand problem. I'm willing to move forward as long as you come with me."

"I'll be there." She climbed on top of me.

"You have any money for furniture?"

"No. I told you Remi took the bag. Don't worry though. I got a plan."

"Whatever you do, make sure you come home."

"What's up Nelly?" She smiled. It wasn't like her to be sentimental.

"I'm pregnant and yes the baby is yours." I sat up on my elbows.

"Really?" I was excited as hell.

"Yea. They told me at the hospital. I wasn't going to mention it but since we're in a good space, I want us to be a family." She kissed me and started grinding on me.

"Maybe we should leave." I told her.

"Whatever you wanna do baby." She rested her body on mine and fell asleep. *A baby*? I had to get money fast if I planned on making it outta here. My kid will need its father and I plan on being around.

✱✱✱✱✱✱✱✱✱✱✱✱✱✱✱✱✱✱✱✱✱✱

"Are you sure no one is here?" Joy asked when we broke into Club Turquoise. Well I still had my key and knew the code to the alarm, so we weren't really breaking in. And yes, Joy and I are still fucking even though I moved in with Nelly. It's a man's dream to fuck sisters, why on earth would I stop.

"We good. Come on." I closed the door and went to Remi's office. Unfortunately, the door was locked so I went down to the manager's office and bingo, the door was unlocked.

"Oh shit, look at this." She pointed to the safe I didn't have the combination to. I went to the drawer I knew Tara locked the money in if it got too late and it too was locked.

"Fuck!" I searched the room for a hammer or something and nothing was there. I went out to the maintenance closet and found one along with a screwdriver.

"Move." I pushed Joy out the way because she was using a paperclip tryna get in.

BAM! BAM! I hit the drawer a few more times and it finally opened.

"Oh shit." We said at the same time. There were two fat ass deposit bags inside. I saw a few gift cards and the keys to other shit. I knew for a fact it wasn't to Remi's office because no one had the key to it. The reason I didn't break into his office is because he had an alarm on it and I know it would go off wherever he was.

"Look at all these twenties and hundreds." Joy said and tried to take the money out. I snatched it from her and put it back in.

"Excuse me. Lets take some liquor too." She walked out and went behind the bar.

"Its some expensive shit in here." I walked up behind her and slid my hands under her shirt.

"Ivan lets fuck in here." She turned and started unbuttoning her jeans. Joy was spontaneous and down for whatever, whenever.

"Why not?" I pulled my dick out and poured some Hennessey on it as she sucked me off.

"Fuck me baby." She turned and spread her pussy open.

"Yes baby. Harder Ivan." She held onto the bar and threw her pussy at me. I smacked her on the ass and looked up at the camera above us. I stuck my middle finger up and smiled. Remi will watch this when he comes in.

"I love you Ivan." She screamed out and came on my dick. We've only been sleeping together for a few weeks. How the hell she love me already? I said the same thing, knowing damn well I didn't mean it. Nelly is the only woman I ever loved, that's why I beat her ass when she mentioned using me. That shit hurt me to the core.

"I'm about to cum." I pulled out and squirted on the liquor bottles and the ground. Fuck Remi and everyone he cool with.

"You bad baby." She smiled and kissed me.

"Hell yea I am. Let's go before someone stops by." We hurried to get dressed and ran outta there. It was five in the morning and Remi came to do the books and make sure inventory was on point around nine. I couldn't wait for him to see this.

Remi

"Have a good day baby." Naima whispered in my ear as she got ready for work. I hated her going anywhere when we had no clue where my brother was but she refused to stay home. I did have someone watching from the moment she left the house, until she got home.

"I'll meet you at the doctors." I laid on my stomach with my head in the pillow, still tired from the early morning sex we had. She took her ass back to sleep where I stayed up watching the sports channel. I wanted to kill Ivan so bad, I had trouble sleeping lately. When I finally dosed off, it was after five.

"Ok. I made you lunch and put it in the fridge." I turned over.

"Thanks, and I have a surprise for you tonight."

"No more sex Remi. Give me at least two days." I laughed.

"How you saying that when your horny ass woke me up?" She gave me the finger and put her shoes on.

"I love you Remi and I promise to keep my mouth shut and be careful." She blew me a kiss and walked out the room.

I thought about going to sleep but decided to get up and start my day. I needed to stop by both clubs to grab the deposits and make it to the doctor's appointment this afternoon. Tara wasn't feeling good last night so I had the bartender lock the money up in the drawer. No one had the safe combination but Tara and its gonna stay that way. The bartender did have the key for days like this. He's the only person I trusted besides my cousin.

I prepared myself for the day and drove to work thinking about all the different businesses I wanna open. I have restaurants but its money to invest everywhere and I definitely wanted to try my hand in different areas. Naima and I were discussing opening up a hair salon. She said women love getting their head done and its always money to make.

I pulled in my spot at the club and went in through the side door. I shut the lights on and noticed the door to Tara's office was open. I didn't see her car outside and I know damn sure no one could get in without a key. I stepped in and instantly noticed the broken drawer. The money was missing and the hammer the person used to get it open sat on top of the desk. I walked out and in the bar area.

"What the…?" I almost slipped on some white shit. Everyone knew how I felt about spilling drinks and not cleaning up after themselves. I grabbed some paper towels to clean it up and felt my phone vibrate.

"Yo. Open up." Cat yelled in the phone. I put the paper towels on the bar and went to get the door. Him and Ivy walked in together.

"Hey Remi." She kissed my cheek and headed up the steps to my office. I forgot she was stopping by to check my books. I let Cat walk up behind her, then I followed.

"Everything is right there. Let me know if you need something." I said and opened the door.

"Ok. Make sure you bring me the finances from last night. I may as well do them while I'm here."

"Oh shit. Hold on." I kneeled down next to her and turned on my security cameras. The place I held the computer for security was in the bottom drawer.

"What's up?" Cat asked when the screens popped up on the other televisions.

"The door was opened to Tara's office when I got here and the deposit bags were missing."

"What?"

"Yea and the person used a hammer to break the drawer."

"Nigga's bugging." Cat said and Ivy shook her head.

"I meant to look but then almost fell in the bar. I was about to clean up the floor when you called. I may as well look at the cameras now before I forget."

I started the cameras at midnight and fast forwarded until closing. No one would go in the office during work hours because they'd be too scared of getting caught.

The video showed the bartender putting the bags in the office, closing the door and him leaving. The other camera showed him and my head security guy locking up and driving off.

"That's weird. He didn't come out with the bags." Ivy spoke the obvious. I fast forwarded more and nothing. It wasn't until after five this morning did two figures pop up on the screen.

"This nigga testing me." Cat had an evil look on his face and Ivy was lost.

We all watched as my brother went in the office, came out and went to the janitor's closet. Her returned with the hammer and screwdriver and shortly after emerged from the office with the bags. What he did next had me fuming; especially, knowing I was about to clean it up. I chuckled at him stick his finger up because he knew I'd watch it. I zoomed in on the chick and smirked. I knew exactly who she was.

"Umm, you ok?" Ivy asked.

"Yup. Do the books and I'll check the registers for the total. I replace the money with my own. That way my balance won't be off." She nodded and started working.

"What time we going there?" Cat asked already knowing what was going on in my head.

"After I go to the doctor's appointment with Naima."

"How did he get in?"

"Its my fault. I was supposed to change the locks and forgot. It's all good because his time is coming."

****

"How are you Remi? I haven't seen you in a very long time." Nelly's mom said when I pulled up in her daughter's driveway. She always said Nelly messed up when she started messing with my brother. She phony as hell though because Ivan was giving her freeloading ass money too.

"I'm good. Is Joy home?"

"No, she ran to the store. If you wait, she'll be back soon."

"I'll come back another day." I pulled out behind her and pretended to leave. After I kill this bitch, I don't want her mom saying I was here waiting on her.

I parked down the street and walked up to her house with Cat. I put my gloves on and kicked the door in. I didn't do it too hard because I wanted her to come in. If it were off the hinges, she'd probably contact the police.

"Look at this shit." Cat held up one of the liquor bottles from my club. I knew it was mine because she had it in her hand on video.

"This bitch is dirty." I kicked over the take-out box she left on the floor.

"He's definitely fucking her." Cat pointed to the bedroom and the clothes he had on last night were in a corner. The two of us searched the other rooms looking for Ivan and he was nowhere in sight.

"What the hell?" I heard and leaned on the wall looking at her. Joy was pretty like her sister, but she's always been a ho. I'm sure she knew about Ivan and Nelly and here she was sleeping with him too.

"What's poppin Joy?" She looked up and tried to haul ass. Cat caught her by the hair and drug her to the couch.

"You thought that shit was funny you and my brother did at the club?"

"Remi, he made me come with him." I pushed my body off the wall and walked towards her.

"He made you suck his dick and fuck behind my bar?" She didn't say anything.

"I didn't see him forcing you to do anything. Actually, weren't you the one picking up bottles and smiling?" I pulled the gun out my waist.

"Please don't kill me."

"Where is he?" I cocked my gun and placed it on her forehead.

"I don't know. He was staying here and after we left your club, he dropped me off and left." I snickered.

BAM! I hit her on the head with the butt of the gun. I hated to put my hands on a woman, but the ones I did hit, were enemies.

"AHHHHH!" She screamed out.

"His clothes are in your room. Let's try this again. Where is he?"

"I don't know."

"Wrong answer but don't worry. I'm gonna find him even after your death."

"Huh?"

PHEW! Her body slumped over on the couch. I found a pen and picked up one of the napkins on the coffee table.

I'm coming for you Ivan.

Is all I wrote and left out the front door with my real brother. Ivan thinks he has one up on me, but I'm almost positive I know where he is. I'm gonna give him a few more days and then, I'm taking his life.

I have a surprise for my girl and I didn't want it ruined because my brother was dead. I was gonna have to comfort my mother because at the end of the day, she's going to be hurt. Ivan better live his days like it's his last.

Naima

"Bitch, it was disgusting what they did. I mean, if it was his club and his girl then ok but it wasn't. Then, he shot his cum on the floor and on his liquor bottles." I had my face turned up listening to Ivy explain what happened at Remi's club. We were having our usual Friday night drinks, only it was soda and we were at this Italian restaurant. I was in the mood for chicken marsala and a nice salad.

Remi came to the doctor's appointment upset but didn't mention what happened. He planned a surprise and canceled that too. After hearing what she witnessed on the tape, I don't blame him. I would've probably thrown up if I saw the video. I've heard of family members being jealous over their siblings, but Ivan takes the cake. He was trying any and everything to destroy my man.

"Its sad when a man has to go through all that for attention." Ivy gave me a look.

"Bitch, don't try me." I said and ate some food.

"I'm just saying you were doing too much at one point too. Tryna play super woman and *I don't need no help shit*." I sucked my teeth.

"I thought Nyeemah was gonna beat that ass. Girl you were pushing it for real." I waved her off. I apologized to my mother and thankfully she accepted. Some parents hold a grudge and I'm glad she didn't.

"Anyway, you wanna drive with me up north to Short Hills mall? They have this purse in Chanel I want."

"I hate taking the ride but they do have nice shit out there. I guess." Her phone rang and Cat's name popped up.

As she spoke, I went online to the Chanel website to make sure the purse I wanted was still available. I wasn't too keen on their clothes and only some of their shoes were nice. The purses though were fire. Definitely on the expensive side but nice as hell. As I was scrolling Tara's name popped up taking me away from the site.

"Hey Tara. How you feeling?" Remi said she was sick for a few days and called out the other night.

"Where are you Naima?" The tone in her voice made me alert. It wasn't like she yelled but it wasn't her normal chipper one.

"Out with Ivy, what's wrong?" I waved the waitress over because like I said, her tone made me believe something was wrong. Ivy gave me a confused look.

"You need to get over to Paradise. Something happened to Remi and…" I disconnected the call, hopped up out my seat and rushed Ivy out.

"I'll be right there." I left $100 bill on the table. It was less than that, but I didn't have time to wait for change or get arrested for dipping out on my bill.

"What's wrong Naima?" Ivy questioned me from behind on the way out.

"I don't know. Tara said something happened to Remi and… Oh my God. What if Ivan got to him first?"

"Calm down Naima and give me the keys. I'll drive." I nodded and handed them over. Tears were running down my face and all I could think of is what if Remi doesn't make it? My child won't have a father.

It took us fifteen minutes to get there and every minute passing felt like hours. Ivy pulled in the parking lot and there were quite a bit of cars. I didn't see any ambulances or cop cars which could be because they've already taken him to the hospital.

I didn't want to get out the car but Ivy opened the door and told me I had to find out if he was ok. It took me another few minutes, but I finally stepped out, leaving my phone and purse in case we needed to rush back to the car.

"You ok?" Ivy asked and I told her once I find out if Remi's ok, I will be. She opened the door.

"Wait a minute." I stopped, wiped my eyes and turned to the parking lot. Ivy had her head in the phone grinning.

"Why are…" I wasn't able to finish my sentence.

"Naima, its about time. Remi needs you." Tara said and grabbed my hand.

"Where is he?" I stopped when we got further inside, and everyone was standing there staring at me.

"Shit. Is he ok? Where is he?" I started panicking again.

"Right here." I turned around and Remi was down on one knee. He had a small black velvet pillow with a box on top of it. I covered my mouth and let the tears fall.

"Naima Carter, you came in my life at a time when being in love wasn't where I ever imagined myself. I was turned off from love due to my past and had too much going on. Somehow you had me stuck after our first meet and greet. I don't wanna give too long of a speech but know I love the hell outta you woman and I want you as my wife. Will you marry me?" I turned to my mother who was shaking her head yes. Not that I needed her approval, but I wanted it.

"Yes Remi. I'll marry you." He tossed the pillow on the ground, opened the box, placed the humongous diamond on my finger and lifted me in his arms.

"I love you so much baby." I whispered in his ear and kissed him.

"A'ight y'all damn." Everybody said as we stood there going at it.

"Come here." He put me down and led me upstairs to his office.

"Remi! You didn't have to." I stared at the Chanel, Prada, and Louis Vuitton bags. There were so many of them, I didn't know where to look first.

"Ivy picked these out and said you wanted them." I locked the door and didn't bother looking in the bags.

"I want you more." I started removing my clothes.

"Are you in a good or bad mood?" He asked.

"What?"

"I'm saying if you're in a good one we can go all night and we have people down there ready to celebrate. If you're in a bad one then…" I smacked him on the arm.

"Whatever mood I'm in, you better enjoy every sexual moment we have." I unbuttoned his jeans.

"I do but like I saiddddddd…. Got damn ma." His head went back when I placed him in my mouth.

"I love you Naima and fuckkkkk…" He couldn't even get his words out as I devoured him like a meal.

"You can't have cum on your breath. Get up." He had me stand, bend over and did me so good, I laid on the couch right after.

"We gotta go back downstairs." Remi passed me some mouthwash.

"I don't want to." I held my hand out and observed the ring. It was beautiful and never in a million years did I think I'd marry anyone besides Mario.

"You like your ring I see."

"I love it but I love you more." He helped me up and we went in the bathroom to clean ourselves.

"My son is filling you out." He rubbed my belly and kissed on my neck.

"It could be a girl."

"I can't have two ladies in the house. I need my son first, and then a girl." I laughed.

"You are a mess and I'm happy to be your wife." We kissed again.

BOOM! BOOM! Remi left me in the bathroom and went to answer the door. I fixed my hair and checked my clothes before stepping out.

"Naima." His mom came over to hug me, then my mom, Ivy and her mom stepped in too, along with Tara and her mom. All of them gave me a hug and my mom sat me down.

"I'll see you downstairs." He pecked my lips and walked out.

"You excited?" Ivy asked.

"I can't believe I'm getting married."

"Be happy someone wants your crazy ass." My mother said and all of a sudden it became quiet.

"Is everything ok?" Remi's mom came and sat next to me. She moved strands of hair out my face.

"You are beautiful Naima and I couldn't ask for a better daughter in law."

"What's wrong?"

"Ivan burned your house down and…" I gasped because he really hated me over a damn inspection.

"Whatever he used made the house explode so there's nothing left." I looked at my mother because she already knew what I was about to ask.

"They're gone honey, but I have some you can have." I was devastated to learn all the photos of my father were gone. I had a few of his necklaces and some cards he gave my mother. He was a romantic when it came to her. All my degrees were replaceable and so were my clothes, but my father's things weren't. I hopped up off the couch.

"I HATE HIM! WHY DID HE HAVE TO BE REMI'S BROTHER? I DON'T THINK I CAN MARRY REMI." I shouted and paced back and forth.

"WHAT?" I heard everyone yell.

"I don't wanna be attached to him whatsoever. He's like a disease that won't go away." I looked at Remi's mother.

"I'm sorry Mrs. Stevens but I hope Ivan dies."

"NAIMA CARTER. YOU FUCKING APOLOGIZE RIGHT NOW TO HER." My mother shouted and she stood.

"Its ok Nyeemah. She has every right to feel the way she does. I'm sure everyone in this room feels some way towards Ivan." She stood in front of me and I noticed Tara's mom step out the room.

"The real reason Ivan isn't dead is because Remi's been tryna to spare me the hurt and pain I'm going to endure." I put my head down because I never took the time out to realize how much pain she'll be in.

"My son may be hateful, jealous, ignorant and even a horrible person, but he is my son." The entire room got quiet.

"A son who I never thought would do the things he's done to his family. A son I loved so much, I enabled him to be how he is in some way."

"You ok? What's going on?" Remi's father came in and so did Remi and Cat.

"I'm fine. Naima is having a moment because we told her what Ivan did." Remi turned to look at her.

"Ma, I told you not to mention it today. Why would you take away her moment?" Remi walked over to me.

"I want to say this to you Naima and I'll leave you alone." She smiled and took my hands in hers.

"You're about to have a child and I trust you're going to raise him or her the best way you can but remember this. No matter how much you instill right from wrong to your children, once they walk outta your sight it's no telling what they'll do."

"Mrs. Stevens." She shushed me.

"My son is gonna die soon Naima and its nothing I can do to stop it. And at this point, I don't want to because he's become so dangerous to me, I can't take another beating like that." She had a few tears falling down her face.

"Congratulations on your engagement and I apologize if you felt I ruined it." She stepped out with Remi's father following her.

"Can y'all give us a minute?" Remi asked and everyone disappeared.

"What's wrong? I know you're upset over what Ivan did but something else is bothering you." He lifted my face to look at him.

"I just want him dead Remi. He's destroying everything and now all my father's things were burned. I can't get those back."

"Naima you're getting upset over something no one can control. We had no idea he'd burn your house down. Shit, we were thinking it would be one of my places."

"I know and I'm sorry for getting angry with your mom."

"Did you disrespect her?" He gave me a you better not have look.

"No. I expressed my anger, but I wouldn't do that."

"Good. I hate to have to fuck you so hard you couldn't walk and then make you apologize while you're tryna recover." I busted out laughing and he hugged me.

"Remi, she said you're the reason Ivan's not dead." He had his chin on my head.

"I've wanted to kill him a lot longer before you came around Naima and she's right. I was tryna spare her feelings because as a mother you never wanna bury your child." He moved me away.

"After he beat her, I told her there was no other option and she's been tryna deal with it."

"Are you gonna tell her when its done?"

"I have to. She wants to give him a proper burial." I nodded.

"Hold on." He reached down to pick his phone up. I noticed the number wasn't saved and felt a little jealous.

"Ok. I'll be there first thing in the morning." He told the person on the phone. He hung up and led me back downstairs. Everyone was drinking and eating. I asked for his mom and they said she went home. I'll call her in the morning.

"I can't wait until you have this baby because you're a fucking bitch." My mother said and popped me on the head.

"I didn't mean to say it un front of her. Its just Ivan is such a dick."

"Which is the exact reason they're going to get him a lot sooner than you think." I looked at my mother.

"Don't ask questions and enjoy this." She waved her hand around.

"He loves you Naima and even though his brother caused a lot of drama between you two, he appreciates you not walking away."

"He better." We both laughed and joined in on the fun.

Remi

"I'll be back later." I kissed Naima's lips on the way out the door. It was a little after six in the morning but this needed to be done. There was no more waiting.

"What time is it?"

"Early. Go back to sleep." I picked my phone up and headed to the door.

"Whatever you're about to do, be careful. I love you."

"I will and I love you too." I headed down the stairs, locked the house up and put the alarm on. Cat and my father were in the truck waiting for me.

"You ready to get this over with?" Cat asked.

"Its been a long time coming." I told him and looked in the backseat at my father. He may want my brother dead, but Ivan is still his child too.

We drove to the destination in silence. I think all of us were caught up in our own thoughts; especially me. How can I take so many lives and yet, struggle with taking Ivan's? Yes, he's my brother and he's done a lotta foul shit but I thought he'd get over his jealousy and move on. Nope. He had to continue being the asshole he's always been known as.

Even if I decided to leave him alone and let him live, my mother and Naima would live in constant fear and I can't have that. I want them to be free and walk around without being paranoid and they can't with him being alive.

Cat stopped a few houses down from the house we were going to and parked. My pops blew his breath loud in the back seat and I rubbed my temples to get my mind right. Shit, even Cat was stressing over it. He's known us since kids and considered us as his brothers. None of us were ready for this but it had to be done.

We stepped out the truck and walked to the house like we belonged there. The door was unlocked like Nelly said it would be.

See, after I killed Joy, Ivan is the one who found her. He also found the note and went straight to Nelly. He blamed her for it and beat her up again but not as bad. Evidently, she was pregnant by him. However; he made her lose the baby and I guess its when she had enough.

She called me at my office and told me he was staying with her and if I could come get him. I had an idea he was with her but because she moved it took me a while to find her. The same day she contacted me, I had already made plans to go there. It helped that we didn't have to kick doors down and chase him.

We stepped in the apartment, closed the door and I placed the silencer on my gun. The place wasn't big and you could tell Nelly was tryna find a place quick after getting kicked out the place Ivan had for her. She was used to the finer things and this small apartment is a step down. Oh well.

My father opened the door and Nelly was up watching television. She got out the bed fully dressed. Her face was fucked up and she moved in slow motion.

"GET UP BOY!" My father barked and Ivan jumped. He turned over, looked at the three of us and rolled back over. He put the pillow on his head and pretended we weren't there. I didn't have to say a word because Cat drug him out the bed by his ankles. Ivan's head hit the floor hard as hell.

"What the fuck y'all? Shit." I laughed. Was this nigga really mad we woke him up?

"You wanna die here or somewhere else?" I said in a calm voice. Ivan knew like everyone else if I'm calm it's not a good thing.

"Where's my mother?"

BAM! My father kicked him hard as hell in the stomach.

"The mother you brutally attacked? Oh, she's home setting up your services. Now, like I asked before. Do you wanna die here or somewhere else?"

"Fuck you! Where's my mother?"

"Right here." We turned and my mom was standing there with tears rushing down her face.

"What are you doing here?" My pops asked.

"I told her where we'd be." Cat and my father stared at me.

"Ivan is her son and she brought him in this world and wanted to be here when he was taken out."

"You always did what she asked." Ivan said shaking his head.

"She's my mother Ivan just like she's yours."

"Whatever."

"What I don't understand is why you're like this. You had every opportunity I had and decided to go the other way. We gave you everything thinking you'd be happy, but nothing was ever good enough for you. You wanted more. You needed more to feel validated. When things didn't go your way, you lashed out and this last time when you attacked our mother, I had enough." I told him.

"So you're gonna let him kill me ma? Your son." He was rubbing it on thick. I told my mother to expect it.

"I only came to make sure you saw me before your life was taken. I wanted you to see your beating didn't break me. I survived and its unfortunate my other son, your brother is going to be the one to take your life." My mom shook her head.

"Fuck all y'all. You never wanted me in this family. I hate all of you." I walked over and placed my gun on his temple.

"You are my older brother and I love you more than you could ever know and whether you believe it or not, this is gonna hurt." Ivan looked at me. I had a few tears falling down my face along with everyone else.

"I love you brother, but it has to be this way." Holding a gun to my brother's head was killing me. I would've never thought I'd have to take my own flesh and blood.

"I'm sorry." Were his last words.

PHEW! His body fell over and my mother fell to her knees crying.

"Why couldn't you get it together Ivan?" She had his head on her lap rocking back and forth. I sat on the edge of the bed, Cat was leaning against the wall and my father had a sad look on his face as he stared at my mother.

None of us moved and stayed there as my mom cried her eyes out. I know it wasn't a good idea for her to come but she begged me to see him take his last breath. She didn't want him to die and be calling out for her like he did. I don't think I'd wanna see something like that, but my mom is very strong.

"What the fuck?" We stepped out the bedroom and Nelly was dead on the floor. She had a single bullet in her head. None of us even heard the gunshot.

"I didn't trust her. She would've tried to blackmail you for money or sex and I'm not having it. Nobody is going to have you but me." Naima said standing there with her arms folded. My father looked at me and started laughing.

"I'ma fuck Ivy up." Cat took the gun outta my fiancés hand. It had a silencer on it which is why we didn't hear it. It was the gun he gave Ivy after Wendy tried to bury her alive, and the one she shot Monee's brother with when he broke in.

"Are you ok Mrs. Stevens?" Naima asked and they embraced each other. The blood on my mom didn't bother her as they stood there for a good two minutes.

"Yea. This is the address." I told my people who were coming to clean the mess.

"I have to wait for them to get here. I'll be home right after." I grabbed Naima's hand and went to her car.

"Are you ok?" She pecked my lips.

"Its gonna be hard but I will be." She sat down, put her seatbelt on and blew me a kiss as she drove away.

"Thank you son." My mom came up behind me.

"Anything for you ma." She smiled and walked off with my pops. I turned to Cat who was yelling at Ivy one minute and then his tone changed. Knowing her she promised him the same thing Naima promises me in order to calm me down. *Good sex!*

"Its finally over." Cat said and hung the phone up.

"Yea. Its it crazy to say I'm gonna miss him?" I asked.

"Nah. I will too. He was a pain in the ass and had he not been so got damn jealous, he would've made a good boss somewhere." We looked at each other.

"SIKE!" We shouted at the same time.

The clean up people got there a half hour later, handled their business and afterwards Cat and I took our ass home to be with our women. Its been a long road tryna find happiness but I'm happy Naima stayed by my side the whole time. Most women would've been left, and I appreciated the fuck outta her for not. We have to work on her attitude but overall, she's a good woman and I can't wait to spend the rest of my life with her.

The End

Thank you all for continuing to support me. I am forever grateful and humbled. I appreciate you more than you know.

Also, my re-releases will drop. I have covers for some but the books need to be re-edited which is why its taking time. Please be patient because they are coming.

Thank you all again. Tina J